Sara was eight when the bombs began falling. The night before she was sent away to Canada, in July, 1940, one bomb hit the church tower in Peterstone.

The next morning, Sara said goodbye to everything she loved, and to her mother and father, who were staying at home to fight the Nazis.

Hours later she stood among hundreds of other children on a dock in Liverpool. She was an "evacuee." But instead of the forlorn journey she'd feared, Sara had adventures. She found a hiding place in a lifeboat and, hanging between the two metal beams that held it, sighted a school of dolphins alongside the ship. She won a battle for independence from her guardian, gruff and snobbish Lady Drume. And she made two best friends, Maggie and Ernie, who like herself were sent away because England was under attack. Together they almost forgot about the war. Almost. Then the ship was torpedoed by a German sub . . .

All the Children
Were Sent Away

All the Children Were Sent Away

A NOVEL BY
Sheila Garrigue

BRADBURY PRESS   SCARSDALE, NEW YORK

FOR
ANN TOBIAS
who gave me courage

Contents

PROLOGUE

ONE Summer Lightning 3

TWO Clickety-Clack, Never Come Back 12

THREE Remember the Nightingale 26

FOUR Lady Drume 36

FIVE Ernie and Maggie 42

SIX Rough Seas 53

SEVEN Lifeboat Number Sixteen 64

EIGHT The Runaway 76

NINE Attack 86

TEN An Apple for the Doctor 97

ELEVEN A German Helmet 105

TWELVE Taffy's Galley 111

THIRTEEN Bird's Eye View 119

FOURTEEN Fogbank 132

FIFTEEN Goodbyes 143

SIXTEEN Tracks 147
SEVENTEEN Fever 156
EIGHTEEN Homecoming 164
EPILOGUE

All the Children
Were Sent Away

PROLOGUE

Sara had read the letter twelve times. She knew it by heart and yet she could not pass the table where it lay without picking it up and reading it again.

Vancouver, B.C.
June 6, 1940

Dear Kate,

The news of the British retreat from Dunkirk has just come over the radio. You're so close to the coast in Peterstone that we're dreadfully worried about you. Surely the Germans will try to cross the Channel soon.

You must make up your minds to leave now, before it's too late. Come to us. We have plenty of room and can help you make a fresh start. But if you and Don feel you can't leave England, then at least send us Sara.

1

Please let me do this for you. It is maddening that this bad leg of mine is keeping me out of the fight. But I'll be more resigned to it if I can feel I have rescued at least one of my family. Let us know what arrangements you are able to make.

> *All our love,*
> *Duncan*

After the letter arrived, Sara's mother and father had talked for a long time behind the closed bedroom door. When they came out, they took her hands and held them tight and told her they were going to send her away.

Her mother's face was very pale. "You must go to Uncle Duncan, Sara. The Germans might come any time. It isn't safe to stay."

Sara looked at her father, but he said nothing.

A long time went by while the three of them sat there in silence. Then Sara nodded slowly.

"I don't want to die," she said.

Summer Lightning

Sara, deep in dreams, stirred and then buried her head in her arms. The mournful sound rode through her window on the scent of apple blossom. It filled the room, shattering the moonlit silence. Domino, curled against Sara's hip, widened his yellow eyes and flicked his ears in distress before jumping to the floor.

"Get up, Sara! Get up!"

Mrs. Warren, a dressing gown flung around her shoulders, bent over the bed.

"Come on, darling! You've got to wake up! It's an air-raid!"

She pulled back the light summer blanket and shook Sara's shoulder. "Quick, Sara! Can't you hear the siren? We must get out to the shelter!"

Sara, eyes still closed, stumbled out of bed and began pulling on some clothes. Her mother hurried to the window and anxiously scanned the southern sky, looking toward the Channel for the German planes. Rubbing the sleep from her eyes, Sara joined her mother and stared out across the valley.

As she watched, searchlight beams rose from St. Peter's churchyard and stabbed the sky, crisscrossing restlessly. Sara thought of the other raid a few nights before, when British fighters had met the German bombers above their own village of Peterstone. How graceful the planes had looked, soaring and diving . . . Later on, her father had telephoned to say he'd been among them. He could have been shot down. She couldn't get the thought out of her mind.

Her mother turned from the window.

"Sara, what are you doing? I told you to get dressed! Where's Domino? Find him quickly!" Mrs. Warren headed for the door. "I must get some clothes on. Come down as fast as you can. We must be in the shelter before they come back." She shook her head angrily. "Oh, I knew it was too much to hope you'd get a good night's sleep before your journey!"

The swooping sound of the siren died away. In the sudden silence, Sara heard a new sound, faint and still far away—a low, pulsing drone, and beneath that the rumble of the big coastal guns. Sara knew what it was—the German bombers on their way to attack London, thirty miles to the north. If they did not drop all their bombs on target, they would dump the rest on the way back to the coast. The village of Peterstone lay in their path.

Sara covered her ears.

"Leave us alone!" she shouted out loud in the empty room.

Her father said the Germans wanted "Lebensraum," which meant "space to live in." Well, so did everyone else! Sara wanted to live in their old farmhouse all her life, just as her parents and grandparents had done. She could not imagine some strange German wanting their home in Peterstone for his "space to live in." He wouldn't even be able to speak English! It was silly! But German planes were flying over the house this very minute. Sara shivered in the warm summer air.

"Hurry, Sara! Hurry!" Her mother called from below.

"I can't come till I find Domino!" She looked around frantically. "I know he's in here somewhere. And he's frightened!"

The little room was simple and stark white in the moonlight. It had always been her safe place. But not tonight.

5

And things would never be the same again.

Her father did not live with them anymore. He lived at the airfield. Even when he managed to get home for a few hours, he stumbled straight past them into the bedroom, asleep on his feet after flying twelve hours a day. Her mother was always at the army hospital, rolling bandages and making beds and learning to drive the ambulances. And she herself was being sent away from Peterstone in the morning.

"It's so far away!" Sara had cried to her father that evening, as they ate their supper in the garden. All around them, the robins were clucking in the apple trees and Domino drowsed on the rough stone wall. "Please. Don't make me go! It's thousands and thousands of miles!"

Her father had taken her hands in his.

"Sara. You and your mother and I—we all love this place. I know you don't want to leave it. But in wartime we have to do things we don't want to do. I hate living away from home. You know that. But I must." He glanced across the table. "And your mother—you know she would rather be at home looking after you and me. But because there's a war on, they need her at the hospital, and we must let them have her. Everyone has something they have to do because of the war. That's why you have to leave here and go to Canada."

"But, Daddy . . ."

"No. Listen, Sara. Even if you weren't going to Uncle Duncan, you would have to go somewhere. Up to Scotland, or off to Wales— somewhere far from the bombing. All the children are being sent away. So you must be a good soldier, sweetheart, and do what must be done."

Sara sighed, remembering. She heard a faint mew from behind the dressing-table. Stooping quickly, Sara pulled Domino out of his hiding place and gathered him up into her arms. She hitched her gasmask onto her shoulder and ran down the stairs.

Together, she and her mother made their way into the quiet garden. To the north, the starry sky flared abruptly and then darkened again.

"It looks like summer lightning," Sara said.

"I wish it were!" Her mother's face was grim. "London's really catching it tonight!"

Far off, a series of dull thuds sounded, each a little louder than the last. The sky flickered, lit up and then darkened again, and the darkness seemed blacker than before.

"Do you think Daddy is up there, too?" Sara asked in a small voice.

"I don't think so. I think he would only just be getting back to the base now. We are lucky he was given those few hours to say goodbye to you! He may not have to go up tonight," her mother answered. But she glanced anxiously at the sky.

Behind them, the dark house huddled against the hillside. At the bottom of the long garden, the moonlight revealed the rounded hulk of the shelter, sunk into the ground. They hurried down the short incline to its entrance and, pushing aside the sandbags, made their way inside.

"I feel like a fox going to earth!" said Mrs. Warren, trying to laugh.

The scent of the apple blossoms could not penetrate the dank air of the shelter. Instead, Sara was conscious of a flat, chill smell, of mildew and moss and mouldering underground things. In the darkest recess at the back of the shelter, the ashen glimmer of mushrooms shone from the gloom. Domino's ears pricked to the rustle of tiny creatures hiding there with them in the dark, but he would not leave Sara's arms to hunt fieldmice tonight.

Lying down on one of the narrow cots, Sara

pulled a damp blanket over her and tried to go back to sleep. Yet it hardly seemed worthwhile when the German planes would be returning from London so soon. And in the morning, if a bomb didn't land on them and kill them all, she had to meet Lady Drume.

Sara turned uncomfortably on the cot, wondering what she would be like. Her mother had found out Lady Drume was going to Canada and had asked her to look after Sara on the way.

"I've never met a Lady before," Sara had said. "Will she act like the Queen? Will I have to curtsy?"

"Heavens, no!" Mrs. Warren had laughed. Then she added thoughtfully, "Well, perhaps once, when you first meet her, it might be a good idea. She's a funny old thing."

"But supposing she doesn't like me? Supposing I get sick and she doesn't know what to do?"

"Lady Drume *will* like you, dear," her mother had replied. "Of course she will. And she is very competent. She has travelled a great deal in her lifetime, what with being married to a naval man. And as far as sickness goes, we met doing hospital work, you know. So she'll know just what to do, whatever happens. Don't worry, Sara." She had patted Sara's hand. "Anyway, it will only be for ten days."

The shelter was stuffy. Sara stroked Domino, who crouched against her, his eyes fixed on the narrow shelter doorway. Suddenly there was an explosion not far away.

"They're coming back," whispered her mother.

They lay tense, not speaking, hardly breathing. Listening. Listening. In a hundred other shelters, every man, woman and child in Peterstone crouched in the dark, listening too. Waiting helplessly for the bombs to fall out of the sky.

Soon they heard what they were listening for. First, a single plane went over, and then several others in scattered formation. Sara wondered if she could see them. She turned on her back and craned her neck to look upwards through the shelter doorway. There, as though hung in a picture frame, the moon sailed in the sky, her face shadowed by the enemy aircraft flying across it. More explosions sounded nearby. Sara felt the shock of them, as the ground shook under her cot. Domino trembled, his eyes huge. His fur stood out from his body protectively.

The silvery call of a nightingale rose from the nearby woods. "Do you hear that, Sara?" whispered her mother. "Oh, isn't he fine!"

They listened as he sang on and on in counterpoint to the bombers thundering overhead. At last, Sara's mother touched her shoulder.

"What do you think of that, Sara! The whole German Air Force can't silence our nightingale once he decides to sing!"

As the sound of the planes faded into the distance, Sara's eyes closed and the nightingale sang her to sleep.

TWO

Clickety-Clack, Never Come Back

Sara felt the faint warmth of the sun on her face as she came slowly awake. Through her closed eyelids, she tried to guess what kind of day this was going to be. Orange and red squiggles swam like tadpoles across her eyeballs. Orange and red so early in the day meant the sun had already burned up the morning mist. It would be hot later on.

She kept her eyes shut, listening to the birds. They sounded so loud—as if they were here in the bedroom with her. Suddenly she sat up and nearly hit her head on the metal shelter roof arching above her. She lay back down, her heart thumping heavily. This was the day.

A sparrow chirped at her from the shelter doorway.

Last time, she thought, feeling hollow inside. Last time to listen to English birds. Would the birds in Canada sound different?

Her mother had already got up and gone back to the house. Domino was gone too. He was probably having his breakfast out of his special blue and white bowl by the fireplace. Sara shivered a little and, pulling the blanket around her shoulders, she got up and scrambled out of the dim shelter into the garden.

Blinking in the sunlight, she shaded her eyes and looked across to Peterstone. Someone had once told her that the village had got its name because St. Peter was supposed to have come to the valley the year after Christ's death, bringing with him a stone from Calvary. He had left it as a sign. Some people thought it was one of the stones in the church's foundations, though nobody knew which one. Her father had said it was all nonsense, when Sara told him about it. But her mother had said, "Why not? How do we know?"

The mist still clung in the valley and the village looked like something in a dream, the outlines of the thatched roofs and plaster cottages blurred and soft. There was mist, too, around the square church tower, curling and rising into the blue morning like smoke . . . Sara gasped.

"Mum!" she shouted. "Come out, quick! St. Peter's is on fire!"

Her mother came running out of the kitchen door.

"Did you say . . ." she began, and then the words faded away as she saw the lazy spiral rising from the church. "Oh, the barbarians!" she exclaimed. "It must have been hit in the raid last night."

They stood side by side, watching the wisps of smoke rising as calmly as though from some farmhouse chimney.

"It looks nearly out," said Mrs. Warren. "The fire brigade must have been fighting it all night." Her voice sharpened as she turned back into the house. "Well, I heard they were going to try and remove the church tower anyway, because it was too good a guidepost for the bombers. The Germans have simply saved us the trouble!"

Sara ate her breakfast in silence. There seemed no point in talking about the things she usually talked about at breakfast-time— school, friends, plans. Her life in Peterstone was over. She had said goodbye to her friends. Many, including her best friend, Ann Palmerston, had left the village a few weeks before, to live in a safer part of England. As far as those remaining were concerned, Sara had already left, too. She was in a kind of no-man's-land—suspended between one life and another.

I don't belong anywhere anymore, she thought.

She choked down her toast and honey, knowing her mother would worry if she did not eat. Questions lay trembling inside her. Not even questions. Feelings. Feelings so vague and formless that Sara could not find the right words to explain them to anyone. Feelings of sadness and fear, and of something wonderful coming to an end.

"Oh, for heaven's sake!" her mother exclaimed crossly, as she dropped a saucepan lid for the third time.

Her mother was different today, too.

One of the things Sara had always loved about breakfast-time was watching her mother move calmly around the kitchen. As she walked to school, there was a kind of safety in knowing that her mother was still there in the house behind her, humming a tune after sending her family off on the day's business.

But this morning her mother walked briskly about the room, clattering dishes and pots harshly against each other, fussing in drawers and cupboards.

Domino crouched under a chair.

He knows, thought Sara. He knows today is different.

"If you have finished eating, Sara, hurry upstairs and get dressed," said Mrs. Warren, whisking Sara's eggcup and plate off the table. "I have told Mr. Parham to come early. We might run into delays because of the raid, and we absolutely must catch the noon train to Liverpool."

Sara heard Mr. Parham's old taxi squeak to a stop outside at eight. She looked around her room.

Her doll, Buttercup, gazed at her through thick black eyelashes from the rocking chair.

"I'm sorry, dear. She's too big to take," her mother had told her a few days before. "You're limited to just what luggage you can carry."

Buttercup is not luggage, Sara had thought. But Buttercup would have to stay here in Peterstone. With Domino.

With a little gasp, Sara picked Domino up from his warm place on her bed and rubbed her face against his body. How could she say goodbye to him? She hugged him tightly against her. Too tightly. With a gentle thrust of his paws, Domino sprang from her arms and ran ahead of her down the stairs and out of sight.

16

The village was quiet as they drove through. One fire engine remained by the burnt-out church, its grimy crew leaning against it, drinking cups of tea.

"Dreadful thing!" Mr. Parham said, from the front seat. "They nearly got my roof too! The thatch started to burn, but I got to it double quick, before it could take hold. Good thing I did! Not many thatchers around these days!"

Mrs. Warren did not answer. Sara nodded, so that Mr. Parham would see in his driving mirror that someone was listening to him. Mrs. Warren stared straight ahead, her face still, her hands clenched in her lap. Squashed in against her, Sara could sense a faint tremble running up and down her mother's body. She burrowed her hand under and into the cold clasp of her mother's hands. Wordlessly, they rode on, while Sara stared out of the taxi window, printing a picture in her mind of every house, every garden, every person in Peterstone.

Once at the railway station, her mother seemed to come back from far away.

"The train is due any minute, Sara," she reported, after a talk with the stationmaster. "It's a good thing we hurried."

The stationmaster said, "Your mum says you're going to Canada. That's a long way away!"

17

"Yes," Sara said.

"I've never been away from England in my life," he remarked. "Unless you count the time I was in the trenches in France in the Great War." Reaching for a crutch which was propped against the wall nearby, he hopped out from behind his counter and pointed proudly to the empty pant leg pinned up above his left knee. "That's what *I* got for leaving England! Swore if I got home safe I'd never leave again." He shook his head at Sara. "Never have and never will!" He turned to Mrs. Warren. "But it's wise to get the children out, ma'am. Much better to have them out of harm's way, so to speak." He wagged his finger in front of her nose. "For those Germans are going to keep coming. Night after night. Night after night. Creatures of habit, they are. Saw it the last time. You mark my words! They'll keep coming back!"

Looking up to see what her mother would say, Sara saw that her face was stony still.

The train arrived. It was nearly empty. Sara was surprised. She and her mother and father had gone to London the year before. They had spent the morning shopping and had lunch in a big restaurant and then they'd gone to the theater in the afternoon. That time the trains had been full of people. But today they had a coach to themselves. Then Sara remembered hearing her father say that London was a place to stay away from these days, unless you had official business there.

She chose a window seat and positioned herself so that she would ride backwards. By leaning forward and staring as hard as she could, she was able to keep the roofs of Peterstone and the old church tower in view for the longest possible time, until the village disappeared from sight around a curve in the track.

The train rolled through pasture land scattered here and there with old farm machinery, placed there to prevent enemy landings. They passed wide playing fields dug up into trenches and anti-aircraft posts. Sara could see the long gun muzzles sticking skywards from their sandbagged forts. As the train neared London, the countryside gave way to rows of narrow back gardens streching away from narrow brick houses. In each garden, the owner had planted rows of vegetables to add to the family's food rations. And in each, like a fungus growth of toadstools, the round top of an air-raid shelter bloomed among the vegetables.

Charing Cross Station was crowded with

troops waiting for a train. While Mrs. Warren was looking for a taxi, Sara watched a soldier whose girl had come to see him off. They leaned against a pillar in the station lobby, pressed together in a goodbye kiss.

I should think his buttons would hurt her, thought Sara.

The kiss went on for such a length of time that she began counting up to see how long they could last before they ran out of breath. When they finally broke apart, she had reached 52.

"Don't stare, Sara," said her mother softly. "It's hard to say goodbye in front of other people. Here's a taxi. Hop in!"

Sara followed her mother into the taxi, glancing back at the soldier as she did so. Her father had told her to be a good soldier. I am, she thought. I'm just like him, being sent away to a place I've never seen. And neither of us knows when we're coming back.

As the taxi began to move, she looked at the soldier one last time. There were tears on his cheeks.

The streets were full of people. Everyone seemed to have somewhere official and urgent to go. Almost everyone, man and woman alike, was wearing a uniform of some kind. Nobody bothered looking in the big store windows. They were bare of merchandise and the huge panes of glass had been crisscrossed with ugly sticky tape to keep dangerous splinters from flying around in the bombing. Sandbags were piled up in front of them. One window they passed had an easel on display, with a poster propped on it. It showed a grotesquely large ear and warned THE WALLS HAVE EARS! CARELESS TALK COSTS LIVES! Sara missed the elegant mannequins she had seen the year before. They had looked so beautiful that afterwards she had spent ten minutes every night in front of the mirror sucking in her cheeks to make herself look like them. A week went by before she decided it was not going to work.

She adjusted her gasmask strap, which was digging into her shoulder.

"Why do we have to wear these all the time!" she complained to her mother. "I'd rather die than put it over my face again!"

At school, they had to wear the cold, rubbery things over their heads for half an hour at a time, filing out to the air-raid shelters like a parade of anteaters, with the long airtubes dangling in front of their faces. When they spoke, their voices sounded hollow and strange, as if they were holding their noses. Sara would have liked to laugh, because they all looked so funny, but laughing took too much breath and she never felt she could get enough air up through the tube. During the first weeks of the war, nine months before, Sara had often dreamed about stifling to death in her gasmask.

Her mother answered more sharply than usual.

"You'd put it on soon enough if there was a poison gas attack!" she said, and then, "You won't have to bother with it much longer. Once we get to the boat, you can hand it over to me. I'll bring it home and turn it in for someone else to use."

Sara fell silent and stared upwards from the taxi window at the barrage balloons hovering above them in the blue sky. They sailed over London like a school of giant silver whales, glinting in the sun, waiting to entangle in their anchoring cables any German plane that might fly too low.

Euston Station was filled with mothers and children hurrying this way and that, looking for the right group to join. Large signs had been erected in various parts of the great main lobby which read CLERKENWELL EVACUEES, BOW EVACUEES, EAST HAM EVAC-

UEES, BILLINGSGATE EVACUEES. Under each sign, a crowd of children stood, eyeing one another, while their mothers spoke anxiously with the group escorts. Each child had a large label pinned to his coat, giving his name and destination. Some held on to a brother or sister. Many clutched a doll or toy bear to their chests. Sara wished Buttercup was not so big.

Hollow loudspeaker announcements echoed in Sara's head. She gripped her mother's hand as they walked past one group of children after another.

"Are they *all* going on my boat?" she asked.

"Yes," her mother replied.

Why, there are *hundreds!* Sara thought.

She stared at the other children as her mother pulled her along. Some were crying.

I won't cry, Sara promised herself. She tried to swallow down the lump that had risen in her throat. It wouldn't do any good, anyway.

She took a last look back the way they had come. Following them onto the platform was a long line of children, each carrying a small suitcase. Their escorts marched alongside. Behind them, beyond the gate, their mothers' faces pressed against the railings. As Sara and her mother climbed aboard the train, the children followed them, pressing around them till all the seats in all the coaches were filled. The children were silent and, sitting down, they stared in front of them or down at their hands. The only voices she heard were those of the escorts as they quietly went about, checking off each child's name. Sara held tight to her mother's hand as she watched the tears run silently down the face of a girl across the aisle.

There was a flurry of shouts and whistles and Sara saw the platform begin to slide by her window, slowly at first, and so smoothly she hardly believed they were moving, then faster and faster.

A long time went by. The train rattled over its rails as it sped northward to Liverpool. Sara sat motionless, sticky in the hot sun which poured in through the thick train window. Her mother was silent and still as ice beside her. There seemed nothing left to say to each other. Sara's voice was locked up inside her mind, where it said over and over again, clickety-clack, never come back . . . clickety-clack, never come back . . . clickety-clack, never come . . . The heavy weight inside her chest seemed to anchor her to her seat. Her lungs found it hard to breathe around the block of iron that had settled there.

The children nearby had begun to talk— quietly at first, but soon their voices grew louder. Now they were running up and down the aisle of the train, laughing. Sara wondered how they could have forgotten so quickly.

She wished she could forget. But all she could think about were the things she was leaving behind. Her mother. Buttercup. Her little white room. Domino. And her father.

Sara pictured him, remembering the hungry way he had looked at her as he had left the previous evening to return to the base—the way he had passed his hand gently over her face—her nose and eyelids and cheek and chin—teaching his fingers the shape of her features. Her eyes stung with sudden tears. She blinked them back, staring out of the window at the telegraph poles flashing by. The tears ran down inside her, and suddenly she felt sick.

Unfrozen from her seat at last, Sara ran for the end of the coach her mother close behind her. Locked in the tiny bathroom, Sara was sick over and over again, as though her body was trying to rid itself of the hurting thing inside it. And, as her mother bent over her, wiping her clammy forehead, Sara felt warm tears splash down upon her head. They stayed there a long time, and, kneeling on the floor of the stuffy, smelly cubicle, they held each other and wept.

THREE
Remember the Nightingale

Lady Drume was waiting for them in the customs building at the dock. She nodded graciously at Sara's bob of a curtsy and said, "Sit down on your suitcase, child. You look pale."

Sara did as she was told while her mother passed over her head the ticket and all the forms they'd filled in, and the blue and gold passport with her picture inside. Her mother's voice was anxious and soft. Lady Drume's was confident and loud.

She has such a *big* voice, thought Sara.

Everything about Lady Drume was big. She had a big, square head, topped by a hairy tweed hat. A big, brown tweed cape. Big, barrel-shaped legs in thick stockings. And big, flat feet in boat-like shoes. Her voice boomed over Sara's head. Even with the crash of the luggage carts echoing around them, Sara was

26

sure everybody else in the huge customs shed was listening to them. She knew she had seen some of the children from the train grinning at her, as they were herded past on their way to the ship.

"Say goodbye to your mother. There's a good girl!"

Sara jumped as Lady Drume spoke to her. Then she turned to her mother, but her throat was tight with tears. Mrs. Warren held her by the shoulders and looked straight into her eyes. Locked together for a moment, they listened to each other's thoughts. Then her mother said, "Goodbye, darling. Think of us every single day. Think of Daddy and me and think of Domino and Peterstone." Her grip tightened. "Sometimes you will feel sad and far away, and things will not go well for you. When that happens, remember the nightingale we listened to together last night. And I will, too."

Glancing over at Lady Drume, who stood a short distance away, signalling for porters, Mrs. Warren frowned anxiously. "Be a good girl, Sara. Do as you're told. Try not to be a nuisance to Lady Drume. And . . . and . . ." Her voice thinned out.

She hugged Sara to her so hard that it hurt,

and then pushed her almost roughly toward Lady Drume.

"I must be going or I will miss my train back to London," she said in a strange, flat voice that Sara had never heard before. "Here she is. Take her!"

Turning abruptly away, she hurried toward the distant door of the shadowy customs shed.

Sara stared after her, longing to run after her, so that they could walk out together and catch the train home. This huge, draughty building, the strangers hurrying all around her, Lady Drume—all these seemed like a nightmare from which she longed to wake up and find herself in her own bedroom in Peterstone. But her mother's figure, getting smaller and smaller, was real enough and soon it reached the door, stood for a moment against the gray Liverpool light, and was gone.

Sara could not turn away from that empty doorway, feeling that, once she did, she would cut the link between herself and her home forever.

Lady Drume bustled up to Sara. Two elderly porters hovered behind her.

"Come, come, child. Don't stand mooning about! We'd better get on board and get settled in our cabin. Thank heavens I've managed to find some porters. You'll have to carry your own case, won't you. They'll have their hands full with my things. Never mind. You look like a sturdy girl!"

Before Sara knew it, she was standing alone beside her suitcase. Lady Drume had swept away without a backward glance and was already halfway down the customs shed.

She is not going to wait for me! Sara realized at last.

Bending, she tugged at the handle of her suitcase and, dragging it along as best she could, tried to catch up. Passengers and porters crowded in front of her as she ran, hiding Lady Drume among the shifting figures ahead. Her arms felt as though they were coming out of their sockets and her heart pounded with fear. But she did not dare pause to rest. At last, she caught a glimpse of Lady Drume on a ramp which led upward to the deck of a great, gray ship—H.M.S. Duke of Perth.

At the top of the ramp, Lady Drume turned to survey the scene below her. Sara struggled up the ramp breathlessly, hauling her case behind her.

"Ah, there you are, Sara! Do try to be alert and keep up!" Lady Drume turned to the officer who was waiting to check their documents. "Who can direct me to my cabin, young man?" she demanded.

The officer signalled an old sailor standing behind him.

"Mickleby here will take you to your cabin, madam."

Lady Drume turned to the sailor. "Cabin 110, my man."

He touched his forehead respectfully.

"Yes, madam. Here, miss. Let me take that bag from you." He smiled at Sara, who handed him her suitcase with relief. "Cabin 110. That would be on A Deck, on the port side."

"Glad to hear it!" remarked Lady Drume. "Port out, starboard home. That is what I am accustomed to!"

"Yes, madam."

The sailor led them along the deck and down some stairs, the porters following along behind with Lady Drume's luggage. The narrow corridors stretched away ahead of them as straight as railway tracks. Doors opened off them every few feet on either side. Halfway along the third corridor, the sailor stopped and opened a door.

"Here we are, madam. Cabin 110." He put down Sara's bag. "You've got a nice porthole to look out of, miss."

"Yes, yes!" interrupted Lady Drume. "That will be all. You may go."

The sailor touched his cap and left.

Lady Drume turned to Sara.

"I imagine you have done no travelling abroad, child. Let me give you some advice. It has been my experience that it does not do to become familiar with the crew. Before you know it, they are taking advantage of you! They give far poorer service. And I have sometimes known them to become quite impertinent! They get above themselves."

"Yes, Lady Drume," said Sara. But she wanted to talk to the sailor. He had an interesting face, as lined as a winter apple. I will, she thought, if I get a chance.

Lady Drume pulled some papers out of her handbag.

"Now I have some business to attend to. You get your things unpacked and wait for me here. You are not to wander about by yourself. Do you understand?"

Sara nodded.

Lady Drume strode out, leaving Sara alone in the tiny room.

She sat down on the lower bunk and looked around. There was not much to see. Two bunks, one upper, one lower. A chest of drawers. A cupboard with folding doors. In the adjoining little room, a small washbasin, a toilet and a triangular bath built into one corner. Sara looked at the porthole and, remembering the sailor's words, stood on tiptoe to peer out. But she was too short. All she could see was the gray sky and a seagull wheeling by.

As she stood there, the ship began to hum. Sara knew from the shouts of the longshoremen coming through the porthole that her long journey from home was about to begin.

Where was her mother now, she wondered. Probably about ready to get on the train to go home to Peterstone. Only five miles away from her at the railway station, but it might as well be five thousand.

Sara turned abruptly to her suitcase and began putting away her clothes in the chest of drawers. It didn't take long at all.

When she was done, she climbed up the straight ladder at the end of the bunk and crawled along till she got to the pillow. She lay on her back and stared at the ceiling just above her head. The ship was throbbing like a live thing and she heard lots of children run past the open cabin door. She wondered where they were going, but she was afraid that, if she followed them to find out, she'd never find her way back to the cabin.

There was a tap at the door.

"Yes?" Sara answered.

The old sailor stuck his head around the door.

"Lady Drume here? Purser wants to see her."

"Who? Oh. She's not here. She went . . . somewhere. I don't know where . . ." answered Sara.

"What are you doing in here, all by yourself? Don't you want to come up on deck and watch us weigh anchor?"

"Lady Drume told me not to walk around by myself," Sara replied.

"Well, then, I'll take you up. You won't be by yourself if you're with me, will you? He grinned in a friendly way. "I've got to take a message up to the bo'sun. You can watch from there. It's a grand sight to see a great ship weigh anchor. You shouldn't miss it!"

Sara jumped down, smiling. He took her hand and together they swung down the passageway.

"What's your name, miss?" asked the sailor.

"Sara Elizabeth Warren."

"And how old are you, Sara Elizabeth Warren?"

"Eight. Eight last February."

"I thought as much. I'm pretty good at guessing people's ages—had lots of experience. Mind you, my own eight-year-old grew up a long time ago. He's off in the Navy, on a destroyer. Good old Wilf!" The sailor nodded as they headed up a staircase. "Named him after me, my Doris did. Wilfrid Horace Mickleby. But nobody calls me Wilf. Everyone calls me Sparky, because I like fiddling about with radios in my spare time."

"Would you like me to call you Sparky?" Sara asked, shyly.

"I'd be offended if you didn't, Miss Sara!"

They walked the length of another narrow corridor and, in a few more moments, came out on deck, high above the wharf.

"This is the bow," Sparky said. "It's the best place to watch from. Wait here. I won't be a jiffy."

Sara leaned over the ship's rail and watched the sailors hurry about their work below her. They untied the thick ropes that had bound the ship to the wharf, and then sent them snaking through the air into the outstretched hands of the tugboat crews. The men on the tugs never missed them, no matter how fast they came. They secured them, preparing to guide the ship away from the dock and out into midstream.

After a few minutes, Sparky returned to her side.

"Ah," he sighed. "It's good to be breathing salt air again. Nothing like it on God's earth!"

"Have you always been a sailor?"

"Yes. Although I *had* given it up to stay home with my Doris. I'm getting along in years, you know, and she got tired of me putting out to sea all the time. But when those Germans began goose-stepping all over Poland and Norway and Holland, it just didn't seem right for me to be puttering around at home, even if I am an old codger! So I says to Doris, I says, 'Looks to me like they might be able to use an old seadog like me, in view of the situation, like.' And here I am!" He grinned cheerfully.

As they talked, the big ship began moving away from the dock. Sara found herself staring down at a churning strip of dirty water. She gulped and watched the strip grow wider and wider.

"Give it a good look, Miss Sara. This country will be going through hard times in the months to come. Look hard at England now, so you can bring her to mind when you're far away."

Sara nodded. She couldn't say anything. She had not until this moment really understood. It would be months, maybe years, before she saw England again. Maybe never.

FOUR
Lady Drume

"Sara!" Lady Drume stood square as an admiral on the deck behind them.

"Sara! What is the meaning of this! Why are you here? I expressly told you not to go wandering about alone!" Lady Drume's face was very red.

"I'm *not* alone." Sara's voice wavered. "I . . . I came up on deck to watch us leave."

"If I might have a word, ma'am," Sparky broke in, "the young miss seemed a mite down'earted, as you might say, and I thought it'd perk her up a bit to be out on deck watching the goings on. She told me you had said she wasn't to wander about alone. But I told 'er it'd be all right if she was with me. So, ma'am, you might say it was my fault she left the cabin, not 'ers. I'm sorry if I did wrong, ma'am. I meant it for the best."

Lady Drume nodded. "Very well, my man. I dare say your intentions were good. You may go." Lady Drume turned her head, dismissing him.

"Thank you, ma'am."

Sara watched him disappear along the deck.

"Let us return to our cabin," Lady Drume said.

When they got there, she motioned Sara inside. "Sit down, child. You and I must understand one another. You and I must have a talk!"

Sara looked apprehensively upward. She could guess who would do the talking!

"Sara, I realize from what the deckhand said that you did not mean to disobey me. So I am not as cross with you now as I was a short while ago. However, in future, I must insist on *implicit obedience*, do you hear? *Implicit obedience!*"

She went on and on.

Listening to the ranting voice, Sara struggled against a terrible need to giggle. She could not help thinking of the day her father had called her in to listen to the shortwave broadcast from Germany. It was Hitler, making a speech somewhere, and he just went on and on, his voice getting louder and louder and

higher and higher all the time. By the end of
the speech, she and her father and mother had
stomach-aches from laughing.

In a minute, thought Sara, I'll burst. And
then she'll be furious!

She looked up at Lady Drume and nodded
solemnly.

"I am pleased to see you have a suitable attitude, Sara," Lady Drume said. "Now get
washed and changed for dinner. And tidy your
hair. It is very disorderly!"

Sara escaped to the bathroom. She pulled off
the ribbons that held her hair in two clusters
reaching just to her shoulders. Suddenly, as
she began to tug through the tangles, she
sharply missed the brushing her mother had
done only that morning.

"I can do it," Sara had said.

"No, Sara," her mother had replied quietly.
"I want to do your hair today."

It had taken Sara two years to grow her hair
long enough to wear this way. Her best friend,
Ann, had thick braids that hung heavy as rope
right down to her waist. Sara longed to look
the same, but her own fine hair did not behave
like Ann's. It grew slowly and it flew crazily
about her head in the slightest breeze. But she
was determined to have braids some day. It
was nearly long enough.

There was a rap on the bathroom door.

"Whatever can you be doing in there, child! Come out at once and get changed!" commanded Lady Drume.

Sara sighed and put away her brush. It did not look as neat as her mother's work, but her hair was divided evenly on either side of her neck.

She came out of the bathroom into the cabin and stopped in awe at the sight of Lady Drume. She was dressed for dinner in a black velvet gown that reached all the way to the floor in plump folds. Its open sleeves fell away from her wrists like a picture in a fairy-tale. A long rope of fat ivory-colored pearls gleamed on her bosom. They dangled down to the point at her waist where a silver buckle fastened her satin sash.

"Come, come, Sara. It is rude to stare. Don't dawdle. Change your frock quickly."

"Yes, ma'am," stammered Sara, and hastily pulling on a print dress, she followed Lady Drume out into the corridor.

The voices of children in the dining-room surged up to meet them. They sounded cheerful and friendly and Sara peered around Lady Drume to catch a glimpse of the other passengers.

As they arrived in the doorway, Lady Drume

paused grandly. A sea of faces turned toward them. The murmur of talk died down for a moment as everyone stared at Lady Drume and then rose again as each tried to guess who she was. The room was filled with tables—round, square and oblong—packed in close together. Looking around, Sara was glad to see that there were children at almost every one. Close by, she recognized some that had been in the train.

A steward in a white uniform approached.

"Your names, please?" he inquired.

Lady Drume frowned at him. "This room looks dreadfully crowded. All these . . . children! I must have missed my way, steward. Kindly direct me to the first-class dining saloon."

"We have had to do away with the first-class dining saloon and lounge, madam, in order to transport as many people as possible. Er . . . your name, please?" he repeated.

Lady Drume raised an eyebrow.

"Young man, I am Lady Drume."

"Ah, yes. Will you follow me, please," he replied. "You and the little girl will be sitting at the Captain's table."

"Very suitable." Lady Drume nodded with satisfaction. "Lead on!"

They crossed the dining-room in procession, threading their way through the closely packed tables.

"Cor! Look at 'er! Look at little Miss 'Igh and Mighty! Who does she think she is!"

Sara heard the loud whisper follow her and she reddened. Just because old Lady Drume was so stuck up, did everyone think she was too? She turned her head quickly and met the eyes of a boy. He stuck out his tongue.

Boys are *awful!* she thought.

She turned her head and continued on her way. But behind her, she heard a girl's voice say, "Ernie, you didn't oughter have done that. She might be quite nice. 'Ow do you know?"

Sara glanced back over her shoulder and looked at the girl. She had pigtails, not nearly as long as Ann Palmerston's, but they were a deep, shiny red. She looked as though she would make a nice friend. Sara decided to find her after dinner.

The steward tapped Sara's shoulder. "They're waiting for you, miss. You'd better hurry along."

41

FIVE
Ernie and Maggie

There were two empty seats at the end of the
Captain's table and Sara sat down in one of
them. Nobody took any notice of her. Everyone was talking to Lady Drume, who was in-
stalled at the other end, next to the Captain, a
large red-faced man with lots of ribbons on his
chest.

Sara saw that there was a menu lying at her
place.

Oh! she thought. Maybe there'll be sausages
and mashed potatoes!

Sara loved sausages more than anything.
Often, in the middle of a dull school day, she
would picture golden-brown sausages, lying
glistening and steaming beside a mound of
mashed potatoes, with a big lump of butter
melting softly down.

She felt hollow with hunger. She had eaten
nothing since breakfast, not even a sandwich.

She picked up the menu hopefully, as a waiter came and stood at her shoulder, pencil poised to take her order. Sara frowned. *"Artichauts vinaigrettes . . . remoulade de boeuf . . . framboises chantilly . . ."* She did not see sausages listed anywhere. At least, she didn't think they were.

"Yes, miss?" the waiter asked.

Sara didn't know what to say.

"Er . . . do you have any sausages tonight?"

"No, miss, we do not, said the waiter. "However, *if* I may say so, miss, we have a very nice selection, considering we are at war, miss!"

"Oh, yes, I know," Sara agreed hastily. "It's . . . it's just . . . that I fancied some sausages tonight."

She had often heard her mother use those words, and they seemed to fit in right in this situation.

"Just so, miss. Just so," said the waiter.

Sara looked back at the menu. It was hopeless. There was not a word she understood. She glanced up the table, but there was nothing on anybody's plate that she even recognized.

She saw a ship's officer come squeezing through between the tables. He had gray hair and his legs were so long and thin that he reminded Sara of a stork. But a lame stork. He had a bad limp. Arriving at the Captain's table, he dropped with a sigh into the chair next to her. He took a quick glance at her puzzled face and the menu in her hand and gave her a smile.

"Hallo!" he said. "I wonder what they've got for us tonight?" He turned to the waiter. "Good evening, Hornby! What magnificent repast are you offering this beautiful young lady and me tonight?"

"We have some nice roast beef, sir. Or, if you fancy fish, sir, some fresh Dover sole. And I believe I heard the chef say the chicken dish was excellent, sir."

"Good! That sounds more appealing than all this fancy French nonsense on the menu! I can never understand why they don't write the menu in the King's English. Don't you agree, young lady?"

Sara nodded.

"Now then, does anything on Hornby's list sound any good to you?"

Sara looked up at him. Even sitting down, he seemed to stretch far above her.

"I'd like some chicken, please," she said, very relieved.

"I'll have the same, Hornby. Off you go!"

The waiter departed.

The tall, thin man sat back in his chair. "I think we should introduce ourselves, don't you? My name is Wetherill. I am the ship's doctor. If you feel seasick in the next few days, you can come to see me and I'll fix you up. So I'm quite a handy person to know on board ship! What do they call you?"

"Sara Elizabeth Warren."

"Are you travelling all alone, Sara Elizabeth Warren?" asked the doctor. "You're not with one of the evacuee groups on board?"

"No. I'm with Lady Drume," replied Sara, nodding toward the head of the table. She explained how she came to be on the ship with Lady Drume.

"Well, I expect you'll want to play with the other evacuee children. There are plenty to choose from."

Sara looked around for Ernie's table and found that the girl sitting next to him was gazing at her. The girl smiled shyly at Sara and Sara smiled back.

Her dinner arrived. It seemed like a hundred years since she'd eaten anything. The chicken was very good, almost as good as sausages would have been. And beside the chicken was a fluffy mound of mashed potatoes. Well, I got half my wish, Sara thought.

The Captain rose to address the passengers as Sara put down her fork. He spoke of his pleasure at having them aboard, of his long experience at sea, of the war, of England, of victory—on and on and on. Sara sighed. Her eyes wandered again to Ernie's table. Ernie was busy tying her friend's pigtails to the back of her chair. As Sara watched in fascination, he sneaked his hand behind her and tickled her in the ribs. She jumped up with a shriek, which quickly turned into a howl, as her head was jerked backward by her hair.

"Oo! Oh! Ow! Ow!" she cried.

A middle-aged lady sitting at their table jumped up.

"Oh, dear, dear, dear! Oh me! Oh my!" she cried, as she rushed to the rescue.

The rest of the children dissolved into giggles. Ernie looked pleased.

"The young devil!" murmured Dr. Wetherill. There was a tiny smile at the side of his mouth.

The Captain harrumped and ahemed and beetled his bushy eyebrows, but nobody was listening anymore. He sat down. Dr. Wetherill pushed back his chair.

"If you're finished, I'll show you the lounge," he said to Sara. "All the passengers are to meet in there after dinner to hear about lifeboat drills and whatnot."

Sara jumped up. The doctor approached Lady Drume and spoke in her ear. She nodded briskly and returned to the discussion she was having with the dried-up elderly bishop sitting on her left.

"Come along, Sara," said the doctor, "let's be off."

Ernie's table was empty, even though there was food still left on some of the plates. The flustered lady had whisked them out of the dining-room in a hurry.

"The lad did a good job!" laughed the doctor. "No telling how long Captain Moulderby-Jones would have rambled on otherwise!"

The lounge was already quite full. In the center of the room a crowd of children stood in a circle, watching Ernie perform a card trick. Dr. Wetherill took Sara's hand and headed in their direction.

"Good evening, madam!" he said to the lady who had been sitting at Ernie's table. "I've brought you my young friend, Sara Warren, who really needs someone more interesting to talk to than us old fogeys at the Captain's table."

All the children stared at them. Sara smiled

47

timidly. She felt strange and apart. She wanted to run and hide in the cabin. But then the red-headed girl smiled back at her.

"Of course," said the lady. "Sara, my name is Mrs. Bourne. We have been watching Ernest Barker do some of his card tricks. Perhaps you would like to watch them, too. Margaret, come here, dear. Will you look after Sara?"

The redheaded girl stepped forward. "I'm Maggie Barker," she said. "Ernie's my brother. He's eleven. Come and watch him. He's quite good at his tricks, really."

Maggie drew Sara into the circle around Ernie.

"He's a bit of a show-off," Maggie whispered. "Says 'e's going on the stage when 'e gets to Canada. Shouldn't be surprised if 'e did, neither!"

Sara was glad he hadn't said anything horrible to her when she came over.

Maggie nudged her. "That's Rosie," she said, pointing to a round-faced girl with glasses. "She lives down our road. And that there's Donald—'e's from Bermondsey." Sara nodded. "And the boy with the curly 'air is Arthur. We sat next to 'im on the . . ."

All of a sudden, there was a commotion in the doorway. Lady Drume swept in, a ship's officer at her side. Her eyes searched the big room. She frowned as she recognized Ernie, and her frown deepened when she spotted Sara near him. She signalled to her companion, who headed in Sara's direction. Sara wished she could sink through the floor.

"Beddy-bye time!" said Ernie. "Got your dolly, 'ave you?"

Maggie turned on him. "Don't you be so 'orrible, Ernie Barker!" she said. "You know very well you've got your silly old teddy bear under your pillow, so don't you come the high and mighty with 'er. We're all in the same boat, we are!" She turned to Sara. "Never mind 'im," she said. "We'll see you tomorrer. You'd better go. Your lady looks as if she wants to be off!"

"I'll look for you at breakfast," said Sara, and went to meet the officer heading toward her. By the time they had reached the other side of the lounge, Lady Drume was already surging down the narrow corridor like a tidal wave. Sara hurried after her.

"You are to undress for bed now, Sara. Wash your hands and face and brush your teeth."

"Yes, Lady Drume," Sara said and began to unbutton her dress.

"You are to take the top bunk, Sara."

"Yes, Lady Drume."

"And there is to be no further mixing with those guttersnipes, Sara. No manners!"

"But . . . ."

"No buts, young lady. We shall not discuss it."

Sara stalked into the bathroom, her back stiff, her head high. She scrubbed her face angrily.

First I mustn't talk to Sparky. Now I can't play with Maggie and Ernie! She dried her face. Why shouldn't I play with them? she thought. I want to. They're fun.

Thinking about them, she wondered how Ernie managed to be so merry and Maggie so calm, just as if they hadn't only hours before said goodbye to their mother. Was it because they were older than she was? Was it because they had each other?

Lady Drume trumpeted through the bathroom door.

"Do not neglect your neck, Sara. Be sure to wash your neck. Nothing more important than a clean neck! We must not allow the war to affect our standards of cleanliness!"

A few minutes later, Sara emerged, neck scrubbed, teeth clean, hair loosened and brushed to a shine. Lady Drume, in a high-necked blue flannel nightgown, was already under the covers in her lower bunk, sitting bolt upright, with a Bible in her hands. She was frowning at her Bible, as though the words somehow displeased her.

Sara climbed up the ladder at the end of the bunk and crawled in under her covers. She closed her eyes and lay listening to the creaking of the ship. The others would all be at the lifeboat meeting in the lounge right now. She and Lady Drume were missing it. Supposing there was a raid? They would not know what to do. It felt strange high up here in her bunk, with no Domino to snuggle against, no mother to kiss her good night.

Sara heard Lady Drume heave herself out of the bunk below. She did not open her eyes. Lady Drume would not wish to be looked at in her blue flannel nightgown, when they had only just met. Sara lay stiff and still under her covers.

Lady Drume came out of the bathroom and Sara listened for the squeak of the lower bunk. However, there was no sound and suddenly Sara sensed that Lady Drume was standing beside her. She opened her eyes and Lady Drume's large face was close to her own. She reached up and awkwardly patted Sara's hand.

"Good night, child. Sleep well. And don't worry. Everything will be all right."

Sara nodded and gulped and closed her eyes again. After a while, the light was switched off.

It took a long time for sleep to come.

SIX

Rough Seas

Sara came slowly awake. She lay, eyes still unopened, listening for her mother's call to breakfast. After a time, she opened her eyes. A quick tremor of fear ran through her. Where were the familiar flowered curtains, the Z-shaped crack in the plaster overhead? Where was Domino?

She sat up abruptly and found the ceiling near her head. She felt like Alice, after sampling the "Drink Me" bottle. She looked around wildly and then recognized with relief the large figure filling the bunk below her.

Lady Drume lay on her back, arms straight at her sides. The waves in her iron-gray hair were held rigidly in place against her head by large metal pins. Her mouth hung slightly open and a wisp of hair puffed up and down with every breath she took.

53

If Ernie were here, he'd drop a marble in her mouth! Sara thought.

Halfway down the ladder, she peered through the porthole. Outside all was gray— gray sea, gray sky, gray mist swirling. And a darker gray shape, long and low on the water a short distance away. Her eyes struggled to pierce the shifting fog outside the window, and then, as a gust of wind blew it into shreds, she saw that it was another ship, moving along close beside them. In a strange way, it was like looking in a mirror, and Sara almost fancied she could see a girl's face just like her own gazing back at her across the churning water.

There was a snuffle and a snort behind her, as Lady Drume closed her mouth with a snap. Sara turned to see her guardian sitting upright in her bunk, just as though she had never gone to sleep the night before.

"Good morning, Sara. I trust you slept well."

"Yes, thank you, ma'am," Sara answered. "Lady Drume, there's another ship outside. It's very close. You can see it from our porthole!"

"That will be the convoy," said Lady Drume and, without further explanation, withdrew into the bathroom. The strains of "Rock of Ages" mingled with splashing sounds, as Lady Drume prepared for her first day at sea.

Sara supposed that a convoy was another kind of ship, like a destroyer or a battleship. As she ate her breakfast porridge, she wondered about it. She wished Dr. Wetherill was there to ask, but the chair beside hers was empty this morning.

She scanned the roomful of children, looking for Maggie and Ernie. Perhaps they had already eaten and were up on deck.

"Can I go up on deck, Lady Drume?" she asked.

"Yes, you *may* go up on deck, Sara. Pay attention to your grammar, child. I am pleased to see that you enjoy fresh air. Most important! Exercise and fresh air! *Mens sana in corpore sano!* That's my motto. A healthy mind in a healthy body! I shall join you shortly and we shall take twenty turns around the promenade deck."

"Yes, Lady Drume," said Sara, gloomily.

She ran up the stairway, feeling the damp, cool air fresh on her cheek after the stuffy atmosphere below decks. Running to the rail, she stared at the scene before her. The mist had vanished and the morning sun sparkled on the sea. The other ship was still there, keeping pace. Some children jostled her as they ran by. She went along the deck until she came to a place where some iron stairs led down to another deck. Below her, she saw Maggie and Ernie.

"Hallo!" she called out and clattered down the steps to join them.

"Wotcher!" Ernie greeted her. "Here! Have a dekko at that there ship. Did you ever see such a sight? It makes me proud, straight it does!"

"Yes," Maggie cried, "it looks somehow brave, don't it?"

"I know. I saw it when I got up this morning, out of our porthole," Sara said.

"Do you have a port'ole? Cor, you are lucky!" said Ernie. "We're all packed in down below like a lot of bloomin' sardines!"

"Oh, that sounds like fun," Sara said.

"Hey, down there!" called a voice. "I see you've found some friends, Miss Sara."

Sparky stood above them on the upper deck, grinning in the morning sun. "How's life at sea treating you?" he asked.

"It's lovely!" Sara exclaimed. "Only I haven't seen much yet. Of the ship, I mean. I want to go all over it and see everything!"

"So you shall!" Sparky promised.

"There's another ship over there," said Sara, pointing.

"Yes, she's a beauty. Have you seen the others?"

"What others?" they asked.

"The four ships in the convoy with us. We met in the middle of the night. We'll be sailing to Canada in company with them, as a convoy. It's saf . . . um . . . it's more interesting that way."

"Cor! Five ships all going along in formation, like blinkin' planes. I like that idea!" said Ernie.

So that's what a convoy is, thought Sara.

"I 'ope we don't bump into each other in the night," Maggie said.

"Oh no, we're used to it. Do it all the time!" Sparky said. His bright blue eyes sharpened. "Here! Where are your Mae Wests?"

They looked at Sparky puzzled.

"Your lifejackets. Why don't you have them on?"

Ernie and Maggie looked at each other.

"We left them on our cots," Maggie said.

"You cut right along and get 'em!" ordered Sparky. "You mustn't go anywhere without them."

"They're a real headache, they are. They're more of a bother than the ruddy gasmasks!" complained Ernie. "You can't *do* anything in them. You can't run and you can't move yer arms right. Why do we have to wear them?"

"It's a rule of the sea that you wear 'em and,

what's more, I'll clap you in irons if you don't obey!" Sparky said. "Where have they got you bunked down?"

"Passenger Lounge C," said Maggie. "They put cots in for us."

"All right then," said Sparky. "Off you go and get 'em, or you don't get my extra special grand tour of His Majesty's ship, Duke of Perth."

Without any further argument, Maggie and Ernie dashed down some steps leading to still another deck below and vanished through a doorway.

"I'm surprised at you, Miss Sara!" Sparky said. "Where's *your* lifejacket?"

"I didn't know we were supposed to have one," said Sara. "I don't even know if I've got one." She wasn't sure what they looked like.

"You must have. Weren't you listening when they told you about the lifeboat drills and the lifejacket procedure last night?"

"Lady Drume said we had to go back to our cabin right after dinner. So we didn't go to the meeting."

Sparky shook his head.

"Well, come on then," he said. "We'll find your lifejacket and I'll show you how to put it on. All the passengers must wear them at all times."

"*All* the passengers?" asked Sara.

"Yes. *All* of them," said Sparky, his eyes twinkling. "I hope we've got one big enough for a certain person!" he whispered. They both laughed.

"Why did you call it a Mae West?" Sara asked.

"Because she's a famous film star, and you'll look as beautiful as Mae West, if you wear it!" he said.

When they reached the cabin, Lady Drume was just coming out.

"Aha! There you are, Sara. Let us be off!"

Sparky touched his cap. "Excuse me, ma'am," he said.

"Yes. What is it?"

"Ma'am, young Miss Warren has given me to understand as how you ladies heard nothing last night about the lifeboat drills and the rules about wearing lifejackets. So I thought as how you wouldn't mind if I was to quickly give you a run through, like."

"I don't understand. Why was I not informed of any rules?" Lady Drume demanded.

"There was a meeting for all passengers last night, ma'am, at which the First Officer explained the procedures," Sparky said.

"Surely I am not expected to attend some sort of mass meeting!"

"Just so, ma'am," Sparky murmured. He pointed to a printed notice on the wall behind the door. "There are the rules to follow in case of an alert. Let's see. You are assigned to Lifeboat Number Sixteen. That's my station, as it happens. Now, I'll just find your lifejackets for you."

He located the lifejackets on the top shelf of the little cupboard and showed them how to buckle them on. They were clumsy jerkins of rough padded material.

"Oh, I hate it!" Sara cried. "Why do we have to wear them? I feel hot already!"

"The lifejacket fills up with air if you go overboard into the water and keeps you afloat until someone hauls you in."

Sara moved her arms up and down stiffly. Lady Drume took her lifejacket off again at once.

"My good man. If you think I am going to wear that monstrosity all the time, you are quite mistaken!"

"Very well, ma'am," said Sparky. "Er, if I may suggest, ma'am, the little girl should wear hers. You know . . . just in case . . ."

"Oh . . . oh, yes . . . I see. Very well. Keep yours on, Sara," ordered Lady Drume.

There was a sound of feet in the corridor

outside, and Ernie and Maggie, wearing their lifejackets, peered in through the half-open door.

"Here you are! We've been looking everywhere! Are you ready, Sara? Come on, Sparky! Come on!"

"Can I go with them, Lady Drume?" begged Sara.

Sparky spoke up. "I promised to show the children over the ship, ma'am. I like children, and I'm off duty this watch."

"Out of the question!" Lady Drume replied. "Sara is to take her exercise with me. Thank you, my man. Come along, Sara."

Sara cast a despairing look back over her shoulder, as she followed Lady Drume down the corridor toward the companionway leading to the promenade deck. She hitched angrily at the clumsy lifejacket. She did not want to "exercise." She wanted to run with Maggie and Ernie and explore the ship. Why did she have to be stuck with horrible old Lady Drume? If only her mother had never met Lady Drume, so that she could have travelled with all the other children. Her mother . . . Sara knew her mother would have liked Maggie and Ernie. If only she were here!

They began to march around the deck, Lady

Drume's chin jutting into the freshening breeze.

"Now then, Sara. I am disappointed that you make it necessary for me to repeat myself. I expressly told you before, you are not to have anything to do with those evacuee children from London. They have nothing in common with you. No background!"

Sara did not reply. She trailed along miserably. The morning sun had been blotted out by racing clouds, and a froth of white capped each wave as far as the eye could see. The hollows between the waves were black and deep.

"Pick your feet up, girl! Walk properly! Brisk step! Straight back! Head into the wind!"

As she walked around and around the moving deck on the restless sea, with the earth revolving in its turn beneath them all, Sara felt like a squirrel on a wheel. But, unlike the squirrel whose journey would never end, each step that Sara took was bringing her closer to the end of her journey. Then there would be escape from Lady Drume. Once they arrived in Vancouver, she could say goodbye to Lady Drume and hello to anyone she liked, whether they had a background or not!

Sara glanced at Lady Drume. To her surprise, Lady Drume's ruddy color had faded into a greenish gray. Her brisk pace had slowed and her large, rather prominent eyes looked like glazed grapes as they peered out over the sea.

She's seasick! Sara realized.

"It must be nearly lunchtime," she remarked, smiling cheerfully at Lady Drume. "I wonder if there'll be sausages?"

"Oh! Oh! Oh!" moaned Lady Drume. She headed hastily for the cabin.

SEVEN

Lifeboat Number Sixteen

Lady Drume lay on her bunk with a cold cloth on her forehead. Sara ate lunch alone. She had been sent to the dining room with strict instructions to return to the cabin the minute her meal was over.

Sara was ready for the waiter this time.

"Is there anything on the menu you think I would specially like?" she asked.

Like a clockwork man, the waiter went into a speech about the various dishes he recommended. She decided on some fish and chips and, afterwards, apple pie.

She looked over at Maggie's table. Most of the children there had chosen fish and chips just as she had. Feeling her gaze, Maggie looked up and waved. Sara waved back, although Lady Drume's last words as Sara had left the cabin had been, "Remember now! I

64

want you to have nothing to do with those Cockney children, or heaven knows what you will pick up! Look for a good book in the ship's library and bring it back to the cabin straight after lunch!"

The fish and chips arrived. She began to eat and, in no time at all, her plate was empty.

"We had the fish'n chips, too," said a voice behind her. Maggie gave her a friendly tap on the back. "Coo! They were good!"

"Our mum could do them better'n that!" Ernie said. "And you can't get a fresher fish than wot you can in good ol' Billingsgate Fish Market!"

"Do you live near Billingsgate?" Sara asked.

"Yus. Our dad was a fish porter before the war. Now he's in the Army, o' course. And me'n Maggie are off to Canada for the duration."

Sara glanced down to the other end of the table.

"Lady Drume says you are Cockneys. Are you?"

"Yus!" answered Ernie, proudly. "Born within the sound of Bow Bells, we were, so that makes us proper Cockneys."

"*Which* bells?" Sara asked.

"Bow Bells. You know . . . the church bells

at St. Mary's of Bow. In the East End of London . . . Anyway, me and Maggie will stay in Canada as long as the war lasts. Because our dad's in the Army and our mum works in the canteen at the docks all day long and then goes firewatching at night. She can't get on with the war if she's got us to worry about, can she?"

"My parents feel the same way," said Sara. "What do you have to do when you're firewatching?"

"Oh, you know. Sit up on a rooftop during a raid and report any fires that start. Not much to it, really."

"It sounds dangerous!"

Ernie looked pleased. "She just wants to do 'er bit," he said.

"I'm going to stay with my Uncle Duncan in Vancouver," said Sara. "Where are you going?"

"To an evacuee center in Toronto, and they're going to farm us out."

"They told us me and Ernie could stay together," said Maggie. Sara heard a little tremble in her voice. "They're going to find a fam'ly wot's willing to 'ave both of us."

"I'd hate not knowing what was going to happen to me. You're brave!" Sara said.

"Don't you worry none!" said Ernie, with a laugh. "Us Barkers always comes out in the pink! And come to that, our mum says it's the Canadians wot are the brave ones, taking *us* on, sight unseen!"

A bell clanged and the ship's whistle blasted mournfully from somewhere high above decks. There was much scraping of chairs as everyone in the dining room stood up, startled, and looked around at each other.

The First Officer climbed up on the bandstand.

"No cause for alarm, ladies and gentlemen," he said. "This is a lifeboat drill, so that we can practice what to do in case of an emergency. Kindly take your lifejackets and proceed in an orderly manner to your lifeboat stations."

Sara tried to remember what number her lifeboat station was. Fourteen? Nineteen? What had Sparky said? Sixteen. That was it. But where was Sixteen?

"I am supposed to go to Sixteen," she said to Maggie. "But I don't know where that is, or how I get there."

"I do," said Ernie. "That's ours, too. Come on!"

"Yes," said Maggie. "Come with us. Sparky showed us all the lifeboat stations this morning, after you had to go for your walk with your lady. Sixteen is near the ship's 'ospital."

Mrs. Bourne hurried over. "Margaret! Ernest! Come along! We must all go to our life-boat now. Please walk calmly!" She pushed them along in front of her. "Now, you all know where you Billingsgate children are supposed to go, because we went through it before lunch. Does everyone remember? Arthur, pay attention! Rosie, do you remember?" The children nodded their heads.

"Race you," Arthur said. "Bet I beat you there!" He tore off, with Ernie close behind him. "Oh, dear, dear, dear! Don't run!" called Mrs. Bourne.

Sara dashed along with the others, out of the dining saloon, down the corridor, up some steps. She followed Maggie and Ernie through the crowd along the promenade deck. Her life-jacket felt hot and bulky and it bumped up and down as she ran, but she did not care.

Laughing and panting, they arrived at the ship's hospital. Sara had wondered what it would be like. It had a big red cross on the door and the smell of antiseptic hung in the air. There was a little window next to the door and she peered through to see if she could see Dr. Wetherill. He waved at her through the glass and then poked his head out.

"Good day to you, Sara," he greeted her. "Sorry I've missed you at mealtimes today.

Been rather busy!" He indicated the whitecapped waves and waggled his eyebrows mournfully at her. She laughed. He turned to Maggie and Ernie. "How about you two? Tummies all right?"

"In the pink!" replied Ernie. "Takes more'n a bit of rough sea to put us Barkers on our backs!"

"What do you think of old Number Sixteen?" asked the doctor.

The children gazed up at their lifeboat. It loomed above their heads, slung between two steel beams which bridged the deck. It was made of wood and looked very heavy.

"It's not like the boat I went in at the seaside last year," said Sara. "That one was smaller, and square at the back."

"You call that the stern, Miss Sara, not the back," said Sparky's voice behind her. "I can see it's time I taught you some shipboard lingo. The front of a boat is called the bow. And the back of a boat is called the stern. Now, who knows why this boat is pointed at both ends, instead of having a square stern?"

They shook their heads.

"It's so the waves that come from astern won't swamp the boat. The pointed ends split up the waves so that they pass to either side."

69

Dr. Wetherill said, "Well, Sara. How do you like her?"

"She's beautiful!" said Sara. "I wish I could see inside. Will we be getting in it at the lifeboat drill? I'd love to do that!"

"No. Mr. Hobbs won't bother about that. He'll just give you your instructions."

Sara gazed up. Number Sixteen looked so strong, so solid. If she were inside, she'd be like a bird in a nest. Or she could crouch down and pretend she was in a great tempest, with whales and sharks swimming by and icebergs looming on the horizon. Huge ocean waves and German submarines could threaten all they liked, but Number Sixteen would . . .

An officer, standing by the ship's rail with a sheaf of papers in his hand began to speak. Sara unwillingly dragged her gaze downwards.

"I am Petty Officer George Hobbs. I am in charge of Lifeboat Number Sixteen. We think it is a good idea to have a bit of a rehearsal in case we ever have to leave this old tub in a hurry. Mind you, it's not at all likely we would ever have to do so." He laughed. "But we like to be prepared." He gestured at Number Sixteen. "Now, if we did have to abandon ship, this lifeboat would be let down until it was at deck level. Everyone would then line up and get into the boat one by one in an orderly fashion, sit down at once, and hold on tight, while the boat was lowered into the sea. I would be in charge, along with Dr. Wetherill, the ship's doctor, and Able Seaman Mickleby, who is a very experienced sailor." He smiled modestly. "You could not be in better hands, I assure you!"

This isn't very interesting, thought Sara. She stopped listening. Her eyes wandered along the steel beam which angled upward to support Number Sixteen in its cradle above the deck.

The way that beam slants, it really isn't so very steep, she thought. I bet you could climb up it, if you had rubber-soled shoes on.

Her heart lurched. Excitement began growing inside her and she suddenly felt very hot. There were rubber-soled shoes in her suitcase. She pressed her hand against her cheek, sure it must be burning red and everyone would guess what she was thinking.

Mr. Hobbs raised his voice and she looked at him guiltily. He wagged his finger at her and said, with a frown, "I trust that everybody here is paying strict attention!"

Sara fixed her eyes on him and he continued his lecture.

"We will not go through the boarding process, now. The lifeboat would be swung out and downwards very steadily and slowly, so there would be no cause whatever for fear. And if, by any chance, there were to be a slip, we have an ample supply of lifebelts ready to haul you in." He smiled again. "Of course, we would not be on the water long before being picked up by another ship in the convoy, or one of our escorting destroyers. However, the lifeboat is stocked with enough food and water and medical supplies to last a long time. The main thing to remember is to keep calm and follow our orders implicitly. They are designed for your safety and, in an emergency, implicit obedience will save precious time."

Sara thought of Lady Drume. "I must insist on implicit obedience!" she had said.

"Now, I imagine everyone is here," Mr. Hobbs said, shuffling the papers attached to his clipboard. "But I will just go over my list. I always like to check names against faces," he said.

He read off the names of the forty or so people assigned to Lifeboat Number Sixteen. Sara was glad to have her name written down on the list, even though she was only eight. The officer finished reading.

"Well," he said. "The only person missing seems to be a Lady Gwendolyn Drume. Does anyone here know where she might be?"

Sara shyly raised her hand.

"Please, sir. She is lying down in our cabin. She was seasick before lunch." She heard Maggie giggle behind her.

"I see," said Mr. Hobbs. "Well, it is quite important she should attend the lifeboat drill and know exactly what to do in case of emergency. Perhaps we can persuade her to come up on deck for a minute or two, if she is feeling better." He made a sign to Sparky. "Able Seaman Mickleby, be so kind as to go to Cabin 110 and ask Lady Drume to join us, if she can."

In a short time, Sparky returned alone and spoke in Mr. Hobbs' ear. Then, turning away, he winked at Sara.

"Won't budge!" he whispered as he went by.

"Well," said Mr. Hobbs shortly, "it seems Lady Drume cannot be with us today. Perhaps tomorrow." He smiled rather wearily at the little crowd around him. "Thank you all for listening. You may go now."

Everyone began to straggle away. Sara went to the railing and leaned over, gazing first at

the sea churning far below, and then up at
Number Sixteen. The more she thought about
it, the more she longed to be up there, swinging high above the sea. Maybe later, when it
got dark . . .

"What do you want to do?" Maggie's voice
interrupted her thoughts. Then, "Here! What's
up? You look lit up inside some'ow!"

Sara turned to her. "Oh, Maggie! I've been
thinking of something wonderful we could
do!"

"What?"

"Well, we couldn't do it right now . . . but,
later . . . when it gets dark, so nobody can see
us . . . well . . ." Sara lowered her voice.
"What would you think," she said slowly,
"about climbing up into Number Sixteen?"

Maggie stepped back and looked upward.

"We couldn't!" she said, looking back at
Sara.

"Couldn't what?" asked Ernie, coming up to
them.

"Climb up into Number Sixteen after supper tonight," said Sara, trying to look as if she
did that sort of thing all the time.

Ernie's eyes gleamed.

"What's the plan?" he asked.

"Well . . ." said Sara. She began talking

fast, as though she had worked it all out long before. "We could meet here after supper. If we eat fast, we could be out on deck before all the others have finished. Then, we could climb up that slanting beam, unhook that cover on top of it and . . . just drop down inside."

"We'd get into awful trouble if anyone saw us!" said Maggie. "Anyway, I couldn't climb all the way up there."

"Nobody will see us," said Sara. "I'll be lookout. Ernie can go up first. Then he can pull you, and I'll push from underneath and you'll be up easy as pie. Oh, come on, Maggie!"

"I don't know," Maggie said, shaking her head. "What do you think, Ernie?"

"I'll tell you wot I think! I think Sara's a bit of all right!" Ernie replied, with a grin.

EIGHT

The Runaway

Sara headed back to Cabin 110. On her way, she dropped in at the ship's library, a comfortable room with heavy square tables and squashy chairs. She sat in one to leaf through a book and the cool leather against her bare legs reminded her of her father's old chair by the fire. It had been empty a lot lately. Somehow, Sara and her mother had never felt much like sitting in it, even though it was the most comfortable chair in the room. But Domino had taken to jumping up into it. He would circle around and around until, with his nose tucked into his tail, his big furry body fitted exactly the shallow round depression in the leather seat.

"He's just keeping it warm for Daddy," Sara's mother would say, stroking the cat softly. Domino was probably curled up there this very minute.

Back in the cabin, Lady Drume looked somewhat better. She was sitting up in her bunk, munching dry crackers and sipping ginger ale.

"Ah, Sara. There you are at last. I thought you were never coming back!" She nodded with approval at the book in Sara's hand. "I am glad to see you've found a book to read. Goodness gracious! Look at your hair! It is extremely untidy. You must brush it at once."

"Yes, Lady Drume."

In the little bathroom, Sara took her brush and tugged at her hair until her head ached. If only it was long enough to make into braids. Then it wouldn't get into such a mess. She tried braiding it but, although she managed a couple of twists, the stray ends poked through here and there like bits of straw. It was still too short. But another month of good growing would make the difference. By autumn, it would braid properly. And by the time she went home again, she would have beautiful, glossy braids that would thump against her back when she ran. By the time she went home, her braids would be just as long as Ann Palmerston's—maybe even longer, if the war lasted long enough.

Once her hair was smooth again, she tied on

white ribbons, then came out for inspection. Lady Drume looked her up and down.

"That's better. You must try to be neater. You seem to be an untidy little girl."

"Yes, Lady Drume."

"Sit down, child, and tell me what happened at the lifeboat drill. Seaman Mickleby came down here and suggested I come up on deck with everyone else, but I hardly thought it necessary for me to appear. Especially as I assumed you were there, since you had not returned from lunch."

Lady Drume patted a small area of the bunk beside her. Sara sat down on the very edge and told Lady Drume what had happened— what they were supposed to do, and who was in charge of the boat.

Lady Drume heaved a sigh.

"That will be enough for now, Sara. I am afraid this talking has quite tired me out. I shall take a rest now."

She slid her large form down under the covers and placed her head squarely down on her pillow. "You may read your book until I wake up."

Sara sat with the book on her lap. The ship creaked as it pitched and rolled through the waves. Lady Drume's travelling clock ticked fussily on the chest of drawers. From time to time, Sara heard children yelling outside and thought of looking out to see who it was. But whenever she moved to do so, Lady Drume's eye half-opened and Sara quickly turned her eyes back to the book. She was trying to get interested in the story, but all she could think about was the secret meeting later on at Lifeboat Number Sixteen. The afternoon dragged on.

On the stroke of five, Lady Drume raised her head from the pillow.

"Aha!" she announced. "I am better. I have obviously made an adjustment to the ship's motion. I knew I would in time. Our family has always bred men of the sea. I shall take dinner this evening."

Lady Drume rose from her bunk and sailed into the bathroom. Above the sounds of splashing, she sang "Hark, hark the lark, at heaven's gate sings . . . As Phoebus 'gins to ri-ise . . ." Lady Drume was certainly feeling a lot better.

On their way to dinner, Sara noticed that ropes had been strung along the wall at hand height. They must have been put there to hang on to, if it gets rough again, she thought.

The dining room was full. On the bandstand, a lady in a pale green dress sat at the piano, playing a tinkly tune. Just behind her, dressed in a threadbare tailcoat, stood an old man, sawing away on a violin.

"A very nice touch," commented Lady Drume to Captain Moulderby-Jones. "I am pleased to see you are keeping up your standards."

"Thank you, Lady Drume," answered the Captain, pushing her chair in carefully. "We do our best. Of course, with the war on, all the young men who would normally play in our ship's orchestra are off with our fighting forces."

"This war is a nuisance!" boomed Lady Drume. "Upsets everything!"

"Just so, Lady Drume," agreed the Captain.

Dr. Wetherill joined Sara at her end of the table and together they looked over the French menu.

"Any sausages?" asked Sara.

" 'Fraid not, Sara. But there is some roast beef that is probably not bad."

"Is there Yorkshire pudding?" she asked.

"Bound to be. Can't have roast beef without Yorkshire pudding, can we, even if there *is* a war on."

They gave their order to the waiter, who stood swaying gently in time with the rocking motion of the ship. He soon returned with their dinner, squeezing between Ernie's table and the bandstand, where the two musicians had struck up a waltz. Ernie made a horrible face at the waiter and then, turning toward Sara, waved his arms at her.

"What on earth is that boy up to now?" asked Dr. Wetherill.

"We're going to meet after supper," answered Sara. "It's a secret, Dr. Wetherill," she added. "You won't tell, will you?"

"Mum's the word," whispered the doctor. "You can rely on me to the death!"

As they ate, the ship began to lurch back and forth more noticeably. The water sloshed in their drinking glasses and Sara had to brace her body against the ship's lean.

"Sea's getting up again," remarked Dr. Wetherill. "I thought that little calm spell this afternoon was too good to be true. I'll be busy tonight, I'm afraid."

Just then, a strong wave hit the ship, heaving it sharply over to one side. Plates and glasses and cutlery slid across the tables and everyone grabbed to prevent the dishes crashing to the floor.

Sara heard a cry from the bandstand and looked around in time to see the lady roll swiftly across the stage on her piano-stool. As she reached the edge of the bandstand and seemed about to fall off into somebody's soup bowl, the ship righted itself, and she came to a stop.

A smile of relief flitted onto her face. The ship shuddered and heaved in the other direction. Before she had gathered her wits sufficiently to get off the stool, the lady rolled headlong the way she had come.

"Eek! Help! Help!" she cried, her long, bony feet backpedalling wildly in an effort to slow herself down.

The old violinist rushed forward and attempted to stop her by standing in her path. But he was swept aside and, tripping over the pianist's feet, he sprawled in a heap on the floor. Sara heard Arthur laughing.

The piano-stool headed for the other side of the bandstand. The lady's floaty green chiffon dress had somehow become tangled with the legs of the stool and she struggled to free it.

"Oh! Ah! Ee-e-e!" She clutched for the piano as she flew past.

The grown-ups in the dining-room seemed frozen where they were. Sara could not bear to stand still and watch any more. The lady looked so frightened. She ran for the stage— sure that, if she could just catch the stool when it got to the edge, she could make it stop. She did get a grip on it for a minute. But it wrenched free.

Suddenly, from the other side of the bandstand, she heard a yell.

"Never fear! Ernie's 'ere!"

Ernie grabbed for the piano-stool. It pulled away from him, stretching him flat on his stomach across the stage, but he hung on.

"We've gotcha! Not to worry!" he cried, bringing the piano-stool to a stop.

The pale lady, paler than ever, untangled her dress and tottered down from the stage. "Oh, dear, dear, dear!" she twittered. "I must go and lie down at once!"

Ernie, meanwhile, helped the violinist up and brushed him off. Then he sat down to his pudding again as though he carried out such rescues every hour of the day. But first, he flashed a special look at Sara. They were partners now.

Dr. Wetherill stood up as Sara came back to the table and seated her with a flourish.

"Well done, you two!" he said.

Sara's face was red. She smiled at him and then pretended to be very busy preventing her plate and glass from sliding off the table to the floor.

"They ought to have damped down the tablecloths to prevent all this sliding about," commented Dr. Wetherill. "Unusually rough for this time of year. There's quite a bad weather forecast. But you seem to be taking it in stride."

"Yes, I'm all right. And Lady Drume says she has adjusted to the ship's motion because her family breeds men of the sea."

Dr. Wetherill looked up the table at Lady Drume.

"Is that a fact!" he said.

Sara followed his gaze and her heart sank. Once again, Lady Drume wore the glassy stare of someone in distress. She gestured feebly at Sara.

"Come here, child. I need you. Give me your arm."

Sara went to her, her heart filled with foreboding.

"We must retire to our cabin at once. I fear I got up rather too soon!" Puffing a little, Lady Drume heaved herself out of her chair. "Perhaps if you read to me before we turn out our light, it will take my mind off this . . . extraordinary feeling!"

"Read to you *now*, Lady Drume?" asked Sara. But she knew the answer and the excitement that had bubbled inside her all afternoon escaped like the air from a punctured balloon. Her grand plan was in ruins and all because of Lady Drume. Sara felt numb with disappointment.

"See you later?" hissed Ernie, as they passed his table.

Sara shook her head despairingly. Seeing his face fall, she realized something else. He would think she was afraid. Her disappointment sharpened into anger.

NINE

Attack

Clutching the ropes to keep their balance on the tilted floor, Sara and Lady Drume made their way to Cabin 110. Lady Drume vanished into the bathroom. Sara's anger lessened a bit as she thought of Lady Drume's greenish face. She could not help feeling sorry for her. Feeling sick was bad enough, but it was plain to see that Lady Drume was also embarrassed.

Sara poured some gingerale into a glass and put some crackers out on a plate. Then she turned down the covers on Lady Drume's bunk. When Lady Drume came back, she nodded appreciatively at Sara's efforts.

"Good girl!" she said, almost as crisply as usual. "Now I should like you to read to me for a little while."

Opening her drawer, she got out a fat book

and passed it to Sara. Her hand sank beneath its weight and, as she quickly looked at the number on the last page, she was filled with gloom. 889 pages of very small print and not a picture anywhere.

"Begin at the beginning, Sara," commanded Lady Drume. "You will find this instructive yourself." She lay back on her pillow and closed her eyes.

Sara began.

"*Famous Victorians* by Clarence Worthy Wilberforce . . . General Charles George Gordon, of Highland and military descent . . . a noble and God-fearing soldier, arrived in . . . Kh . . . Khartoum . . . to neg . . . negotiate with the . . . Emir Abdul Sh . . . Shakour . . ."

Sara, stumbling over the long words and strange foreign names, read on and on, until her voice began to crack and fade. At last, Lady Drume raised her hand and said, "Thank you, child. That will be enough for now. You read quite well for your age. We shall continue tomorrow. Now get ready for bed."

Sara put the book away and got undressed. After all that dull reading, she felt very sleepy and was not sorry to be going to bed. Just as she began climbing the ladder to her bunk,

Lady Drume's voice sounded from below.

"Sara! I do not believe you have washed your neck!"

Sara climbed back down the ladder with a sigh.

Later, as she lay in her bunk, rolling a little in time with the ship and listening to the creaks and groans that H.M.S. Duke of Perth made as she ploughed through the stormy Atlantic, she thought of home. It seemed very far away now, another world.

In that other world, her mother's serene face was shadowed with fear. In that world, her father had left his classroom for the warlike paths of the sky. In that world, Domino prowled the empty house, searching for her.

I must be nearly halfway to Canada by this time, she thought. Halfway to the new world. In that world, there would be untroubled people, who lived in towns where the signposts were still in place to tell you where you were and the streetlamps could be lit at dusk. How different from England, waiting in the dark for the sound of enemy bombers.

Sara's eyelids closed and she drifted into sleep.

A bell shrilled in the corridor outside. The ship's siren blasted deeply from far above them. Sara started awake, every nerve trembling.

"What on earth is that abominable noise?" exclaimed Lady Drume from below.

The bell continued to ring. Urgently. Insistently.

Sara heard feet running by in the passageway and voices shouting orders.

"Can it be possible they have scheduled another of those ridiculous drills!" said Lady Drume.

There was a pounding on their door. "Lifeboat stations, everyone!" cried a voice outside. The footsteps receded and they heard more pounding further down the corridor.

"We shall remain here," said Lady Drume.

"Perhaps it's a real raid," whispered Sara. "Please, Lady Drume . . ."

"I do not intend to move an inch unless someone comes to tell me the Germans are attacking! And what's more, I intend to complain to Captain Moulderby-Jones at breakfast tomorrow. Disgraceful—disturbing people like this in the middle of the night!"

The minutes passed by. Finally, the bell stopped. No more footsteps hurried past outside. Sara felt as if she and Lady Drume were the only people left on this whole big ship. Shivering, she lay under her covers and waited. For what? She wasn't even sure. A submarine? A torpedo? A sky full of German bombers?

Suddenly, somewhere in the distance, there was a muffled explosion.

"We *are* under attack!" exclaimed Lady Drume. "Sara, quickly, child! Get dressed and put on your lifejacket!"

Sara scurried down the ladder, her heart pounding against her chest. She struggled into her clothes, fear making her fingers fumbly. Lady Drume dressed beside her. The ship shuddered. The cabin lights flickered and then went out.

Lady Drume opened the door into the corridor. There was a scorchy smell in the air and a haze of smoke hung at the end of the passageway.

"There's a fire right where we have to go," said Sara.

"Well, we certainly cannot go that way. We'll have to try the other. Come along, Sara."

Lady Drume charged down the corridor, with Sara half-running behind her. They went up the flight of steps at the end of the corridor, hoping to reach the promenade deck somewhere further along from Lifeboat Station Sixteen.

The top of the steps was burning.

"Can't go that way!" barked Lady Drume. "Better go back the way we came."

Hopelessly, Sara followed as Lady Drume strode back along the corridor. By now, it had filled with smoke and Sara's eyes prickled and watered. The foul air caught in her throat and she coughed painfully.

"Oh, Lady Drume. We'll never get out!" she cried. "I'm frightened!"

Just then, a door was flung open in the passageway ahead of them and a grimy figure sprang through.

"Ernie!" gasped Sara. "Oh, Ernie!"

"I thought you'd be down 'ere somewhere. We was all up at the lifeboat and I took a squiz round and didn't see you. So I says to meself 'Ernie Barker! You'd better make yerself useful and find those two!' I slipped away while they was letting the boat down."

"Oh, I'm so glad you came!" cried Sara. "I'm really scared. We can't get out of here."

"Oh yes, you can," replied Ernie. "It's easy when you know 'ow. And we'd better stop mucking about down 'ere or we'll be for it. There's a German U-boat out there somewhere wot's 'aving a good go at sinking us!"

"Now then, young man," interrupted Lady

Drume. "Do you know exactly how to get to Lifeboat Station Sixteen from here?"

"Of course I do! That's where I just come from! Know this tub like the back of me 'and. Come on. Let's hop it!"

Choking and coughing, they ran through the doorway. It led to a linen storage room. A door on the other side opened onto a stairway that led downwards. On the lower level, the lights were still burning. They hurried past a large kitchen, shipshape and shining, with a whole row of stoves and shelves and shelves of plates and cups and glasses.

"Must be under the dining saloon," puffed Lady Drume.

"Come *on!*" Ernie was hopping up and down some distance ahead of them. He beckoned them on and they scrambled down still another flight of stairs to a gray-painted passageway. Deep throbbing sounds told them they were near the engine-room.

A huge explosion went off close by. Black smoke poured from the engine-room door. Lady Drume staggered and then sprawled walruslike on the floor.

Sara's ears were full of pain. She could see Ernie shout at her, but could not hear what he said. Then, suddenly, her ears cleared again and she heard him repeat, "All right?" He looked scared. Sara noticed a wet feeling on her upper lip and when she wiped it away, her hand was smeared with blood.

"Nosebleed," she said, shakily.

"Wot about you?" Ernie bent over Lady Drume.

"Thank you," answered Lady Drume stiffly. "I merely lost my balance momentarily."

"Come on then, me old tulip!" said Ernie and hauled Lady Drume to her feet.

Lady Drume's face turned purple with outrage. She pulled away haughtily from Ernie and hurried forward. But she had taken only a couple of steps when she cried out.

"Infuriating! I have hurt my ankle!"

She tried to go on, limping heavily, her face set. A long staircase, vanishing upwards, lay ahead.

Sara spoke up. "Hold my arm, Lady Drume. I'll help you. Try not to put your whole weight on it."

"I'll come on your other side," said Ernie. "Lean on me shoulder . . . that's it. We're nearly there. We can make it." They worked their way upwards.

"Must be nearly there," Sara assured Lady Drume, whose face had gone white. "Then Dr.

Wetherill can put something on it to make it feel better."

In a few minutes, they emerged on deck near the bow. They stood for a moment to rest. In the darkness, a couple of small fires flickered strangely here and there on the upper deck near the funnel. They saw men's figures silhouetted against the glow as they worked to put out the fires before they spread. Looking across the water, they could see fire glowing on their companion ship.

"Thank God!" cried Sparky out of the darkness. "We've been searching everywhere for you three. Where have you been? Oh, miss. Look at your nose!"

Ernie began an involved explanation, but Sparky interrupted him.

"Never mind telling me all that now, my lad. No time! Come on!" He started ahead of them, but came hurrying back when he realized they were not keeping up with him. "What's the matter?" he asked.

"Lady Drume's hurt her foot and she can't walk without help," Sara answered shakily.

"Here. Let me take her!" he said, and quickly transferred Lady Drume's weight to his own shoulder. They set off along the deck. At Lifeboat Station Fifteen they pushed their way through the crowd. Sara saw a little boy crying.

Lifeboat Sixteen had been lowered to deck level and the passengers were lined up, ready to board, if they were ordered to abandon ship.

Maggie came running forward. "Ernie!" she cried. "I thought you was gone for good and all!"

Sara could see tears on her face. She touched Maggie's arm.

"Ernie rescued us," Sara said. "We'd still be down there in the smoke if it weren't for him!" She turned to Ernie. "How did you know which way would lead us here?"

"Easy. Old Sparky here showed us all over the ship." He grinned at his sister. "And then old Mags and I did a bit of poking around on our own besides. Always like to know 'ow the land lies, don't we, Mags?"

Lady Drume spoke up from her seat in the hospital doorway where Dr. Wetherill was bandaging her foot.

"You are a brave boy!" she said. "You rose to the occasion very creditably!"

Ernie beamed with pleasure. "It wasn't nothing, really," he mumbled.

He was interrupted by a sudden shout from the deckrail, where Sparky was checking the lifeboat's lowering rig. Sparky pointed out into the sea. The ragged clouds had momentarily torn apart and, in the moonlight, they could see a German submarine wallowing on the surface.

"It's badly damaged, Mr. Hobbs, sir," cried Sparky. "See the oil on the water?"

"One of our escorts must have got her with a depth charge," Mr. Hobbs answered.

As the passengers watched, clustered together by the rail, a destroyer steamed close to the crippled U-boat. A boarding party, shouting instructions and warnings through a bullhorn, went alongside to take the submarine crew prisoner.

An hour later, H.M.S. Duke of Perth was steaming on her way.

Lying in her bunk, Sara tried to sleep. But her ears hurt too much and her nose was stuffed up. Dr. Wetherill had told her it would take several days before they went back to normal. It was Lady Drume's fault. If she had not been so stubborn about leaving the cabin at the start of the attack, they never would have been in that corridor when the engine-room was hit. It seemed as though Lady Drume kept trying to pretend the war wasn't happening, even when it was going on all around her. Well, maybe tonight had taught her a lesson!

TEN

An Apple for the Doctor

At breakfast, Sara sensed a holiday mood in the dining-room. There was a feeling of closeness among them all because they had come through a terrible ordeal together.

George, a boy from Lifeboat Number Fifteen, pulled her hair as he went by.

"Didn't get much kip last night, did we?" he said.

"Wasn't it fun!" said Sara.

"We showed those Jerries!" He grinned.

"Good morning, miss," said Hornby, as he put Sara's porridge in front of her.

"Good morning, Mr. Hornby," answered Sara. "Wasn't it exciting last night!"

"Indeed it was, miss. You won't see that much action again in a month of Sundays! . . . Er . . . may I suggest the kippered herrings to follow?"

"All right." Sara wished Dr. Wetherill was

next to her to talk to, but his chair was empty. "Where's Dr. Wetherill, Mr. Hornby?"

"I expect he's still busy below decks, miss," he replied. "He's had his hands full patching people up."

He must be awfully hungry and tired by this time, thought Sara. I'll take him an apple after breakfast. She took one out of the bowl on the table and tucked it in her pocket.

She looked around for Maggie and Ernie. Some of the other children were at their tables, but Maggie and Ernie were nowhere to be seen.

After the meal, Sara helped Lady Drume hobble up to the promenade deck. "Can't stand not being able to get around!" she puffed. "Put me on a chair, Sara. At least I can get a breath of fresh air. I still have that smoky smell in my nose."

Sara helped her into a deck chair and propped up her ankle. It was a beautiful day. A soft breeze stirred the ocean. The sun was warm on their backs. Nothing remained of yesterday's storm.

"Well!" said Lady Drume, settling herself. "We seem to have taken care of those Germans! Good thing, too. I don't know what the world is coming to, when one is not even safe on the high seas!"

"Can I get you a cushion, Lady Drume? Or a nice cup of tea?" Sara asked. Her mother always enjoyed another cup of tea.

"I am as comfortable as can be expected, thank you," replied Lady Drume. "However, a good book would help me to pass the time, since I am prevented from taking my usual exercise. Go down to the cabin and fetch the book we were reading yesterday."

"Yes, Lady Drume."

"And don't take all morning about it! I hate to sit idle!"

'Yes, Lady Drume."

As Sara ran along the deck, an unfamiliar weight in her dress pocket bumped against her hip. Feeling inside, she discovered the apple she had put there for Dr. Wetherill. The hospital was just a bit further along the deck.

I almost forgot, she thought. I'd better give it to him right now or I'll forget again. She hurried along the deck toward the hospital.

There was still a smell of smoke in the air, but otherwise things looked surprisingly normal. The crew had been busy all night. The burned-out staircase had been bridged and there was a "Wet Paint" sign hung at the end of the corridor.

Sara knocked at the hospital door. A minute went by. All was silent inside. Should she knock again? Perhaps the doctor was busy and she should not bother him. But her mother always said good breakfasts are important for good health. If he had been working all night long, he needed this apple. Sara took a deep breath and knocked again. After a moment, she heard sounds inside and the tall doctor, looking sleepy, opened the door.

"Sara," he said, with a tired smile. "You caught me napping!"

"Oh, I'm sorry . . . I . . . I didn't think you might be sleeping." His face was shadowed with fatigue and there was a stubble of beard on his chin. "I didn't mean to wake you up, Dr. Wetherill. I . . . I just brought you this, because you didn't come to breakfast and Mr. Hornby said you'd been up all night and I thought you might be hungry." She held out the apple.

"Don't apologize, my dear. It was very thoughtful of you. I *am* hungry and I thank you very much."

He limped out into the fresh air and took a big bite. "That *is* good!" he said. "I thought there'd be nothing but coffee for me this morning. By lunchtime, I'd have been no good to anyone!"

In a few more bites the apple was finished.

Dr. Wetherill threw the core far out over the side and together they leaned on the rail and watched as it bobbed for a moment in the tumbling water beside the ship and then vanished.

The tall doctor sighed. "That apple went too fast! I could eat a horse! Well . . . I'd better have another look at my patient." He turned to the hospital doorway. "She's a friend of yours, Sara. Mrs. Bourne."

Sara's eyes widened.

"Mrs. Bourne? What's the matter with her?"

"She got a bump on the head in all the kerfuffle last night."

"Can I come in and see her?"

The doctor hesitated.

"I'll be very quiet. I know how you act in a hospital. My mother works in one."

Dr. Wetherill smiled. "Come along in then."

Sara tiptoed behind him, as he went up to the cot by the wall. Mrs. Bourne lay on her back. Her face was as white as the bandage covering the top of her head and her eyes were closed. Sara peered closer and felt a queer tingle at the back of her knees, as she saw the dried blood matting Mrs. Bourne's hair.

Gently lifting off the bandage, Dr. Wetherill examined the ugly gash on Mrs. Bourne's head. Crude black thread cross-stitched the wound. Sara shuddered.

"It's coming along nicely," Dr. Wetherill said. "She'll be feeling better before long." He put on a clean bandage and straightened up.

Mrs. Bourne had not moved. She lay very still and her breathing was heavy and slow.

"Hasn't she woken up since it happened?" Sara whispered.

"For a little while in the night. She was restless and so I gave her some medicine to keep her very quiet." The doctor checked his watch. "As a matter of fact, she'll be waking up soon." He frowned. "I really ought to take a look at a few of the people I treated last night. But I don't want Mrs. Bourne to wake up and find herself alone. She may be a little confused to begin with."

"I could stay with her!" cried Sara. "I . . . I helped look after my dad when he had the 'flu. I can look after her until you get back. She won't be afraid because she knows me."

The tall doctor smiled. "I see I've found another Florence Nightingale. That's a fine idea, Sara. My mind will rest easier knowing Mrs. Bourne will have a friend nearby when she wakes up." He picked up his bag. "I won't be long," he said.

Sara settled on her knees by the cot. A long time went by. Then, as she watched for any sign of waking, she saw Mrs. Bourne's eyelids flutter and slowly open.

"Goodness gracious me!" said Mrs. Bourne faintly, as she stared at the ceiling. "What a dreadful headache!" She turned her head very carefully and then said, in surprise, "Sara?"

"It's all right, Mrs. Bourne. I'm just keeping you company until the doctor gets back. He won't be long. How does your head feel?"

Mrs. Bourne cautiously touched the bandaged place. "It hurts."

Sara jumped to her feet. "I know what to do. Just a minute."

She filled a little bowl with water and took a cloth off a pile on the shelf. Soaking it in the cool water, she squeezed it out and smoothed it over Mrs. Bourne's forehead.

"Thank you, dear. That feels lovely," murmured Mrs. Bourne. "You're a good little girl."

Every few minutes, Sara cooled off the cloth in the water and then replaced it. Mrs. Bourne closed her eyes and drifted back to sleep. But this time, there was a smile on her face.

Sara kept very still. Her knees were hurting and her back was aching, but she didn't want to disturb her patient by getting up. Finally, the door opened and Dr. Wetherill came in.

"Anything to report?" he asked.

She told him what she had done. "Good!" he said. "Her color has improved."

There was a tap at the door. Maggie and Ernie and Sparky were standing together outside.

"We came to see 'ow Mrs. Bourne is doing," said Maggie.

"Yus," said Ernie. "It's not the same down below without 'er."

Sara told them how she was all stitched up but resting quietly.

"Sounds as if she'll be right as rain before we know it," Sparky said. "How's your other patient? How's Lady Drume's ankle?"

"It still hurts a lot," answered Sara. "She can't move at all without help. She's sitting up on deck right . . ." Her eyes widened in horror. "Lady Drume! I forgot all about her!" she gasped. "Her book! She's been waiting all this time for her book! I've got to go! I've got to go right now!"

ELEVEN

A German Helmet

Sara raced along the deck. Rounding the corner, she looked ahead and her heart sank. Lady Drume was hunched down in her seat, her fingers drumming angrily on the arm of the deck chair. Even from far away, Sara knew she was furious.

"I'm . . . I'm . . . s-sorry, Lady Drume," she stammered, as she flew to a stop in front of her guardian. "I forgot about getting your book. I took an apple to Dr. Wetherill, and then I found out Mrs. Bourne was hurt and I stayed. . . ."

"I am not interested in your excuses! It is plain to see that you are a scatterbrained thoughtless girl and that all you can think about is amusing yourself!"

"But Lady Drume, I was . . ."

"Don't answer me back, miss."

"I was just trying to help . . ."

"That is *enough!* Help! Ha! You don't consider helping me of any importance, I notice! I have been imprisoned in this chair for over an hour, with nothing to do, and no stewards anywhere. And you off selfishly gallivanting about!"

Sara stood silent. It was no use trying to explain how she had come to forget Lady Drume's request. Lady Drume didn't want to hear it.

"This awful war!" Lady Drume ranted on. "It has ruined my life! It has changed everything! Nobody has proper respect any more!" She glared up at Sara. "Look at you!" she trumpeted. "Your top button is undone. Your shoelace is untied. And your hair is in its usual terrible mess!" She made an impatient gesture at Sara's hair. In her frantic race back to Lady Drume, her ribbons had come undone and her hair had blown into a tangle.

"Help me up!" ordered Lady Drume. "I have come to a decision!"

Sara's heart pounded dismally. If only she hadn't forgotten the stupid book. Now Lady Drume was so angry she would probably make her stay inside the cabin all afternoon, reading aloud about Gordon of Khartoum. She helped

Lady Drume out of the deck chair and they went slowly, step by step, down the stairs. At the bottom, Sara turned toward Cabin 110.

"No, no!" Lady Drume snapped. "I did not say I was going back to the cabin, did I? This way!"

She led Sara to what had once been a row of little shops. Now, because of rationing, there was nothing anyone could buy any more, so the shops were being used for other things. The one at the end of the row had a light on.

Inside, an elderly man was dusting off a shelf of bottles and combs and scissors. His face looked familiar and, after a moment, Sara remembered who he was. The violinist.

"Good morning, madam," he said, with a little bow. "Good morning, miss. What can I do for you?"

Lady Drume spoke, gesturing at Sara.

"This child's hair is quite the wrong length. It is too short for her to braid it. And it is too long for her to keep tidy. What's more, she cannot wash her neck properly. It will be far simpler and neater if the hair is cut off."

Sara's breath stopped. Her heart stopped. The whole world stopped.

"Sit up in the chair, Sara."

"No!" she cried.

"Be silent, Sara, and do as you are told!" Lady Drume's face was flushed.

The elderly man interrupted timidly.

"If I might say something, madam . . . I have no experience cutting little girls' hair." He spread his long, thin fingers. "I am not really even a barber. I am a violinist by profession. They just put me in here to fill the place of the real barber, who has shipped out on a minesweeper." He looked anxiously at Sara's stricken face. "Perhaps it would be best to wait until you can take the little girl to a hairdresser in Canada."

"I know what is best, my man! I will not hear of waiting another moment!" snapped Lady Drume. "This child's hair is a disgrace! It has been a disgrace since I first set eyes on her!"

The breath hissed out between Sara's teeth and her heart began to thud heavily in her chest.

"Oh, please, Lady Drume. Don't cut my hair!" she begged. "Oh, please. I've been growing it and growing it and it has taken a long, long time. I want to have braids more than anything. Please don't cut my hair off now! It's nearly long enough and, when it is, I'll be able to braid it and I promise it will be

108

neat all the time. If you cut it off now, I'll never get it long enough again. NEVER! Oh . . . PLEASE!"

"Your hair is far too thin for braids, Sara. Not healthy hair at all. You will have a far better appearance when it is nice and short." She motioned to the old man.

He shook his head at Sara.

"I'll do my best, miss," he said. "I'll try and do it nicely."

Sara was filled with hopeless rage. Angry tears started into her eyes. There was nothing for her to do but sit in the barber's chair and submit to the scissors. Nobody on this whole huge ship would ever say no to Lady Drume. She always got her way and she was getting it now. Oh, if only her mother . . . but her mother was thousands of useless miles away. She didn't know what was happening to Sara.

Sara climbed up into the chair and sat motionless as the old violinist tucked a towel around her neck. Her face in the mirror was white and pinched and her eyes were hard and tragic. If she had been preparing for execution, she would have felt no different.

"Don't bother cutting for a part," Lady Drume said. "She doesn't seem to be able to get it straight. She'll look neater with a fringe."

With trembling fingers, the violinist picked up the scissors and began his work. As he snipped away, Sara's heart was cut into a thousand little pieces. Her fine, brown hair floated to the floor.

"It's like cutting feathers," the barber sighed. "Just like cutting feathers."

Before long, he put the scissors down and took away the towel. Brushing the last tickly hairs out of the collar of Sara's dress, he looked at her reflection in the mirror. Her hair just reached the top of her ears. Stray wisps stuck out here and there.

"Dear, dear," he murmured. "I'm afraid I didn't quite get the line right."

Sara said nothing. She stared into her lap.

"Let me see," mused the old man. "I'll see if I can arrange it a little better."

Taking his comb, he dipped it into some water and ran it through her hair, smoothing it down against her head.

"There," he said, "I think that looks better."

Stonefaced, Sara stared at the slicked-down image in the glass. She might have been wearing a German helmet.

TWELVE
Taffy's Galley

Sara followed Lady Drume back to the cabin. Her hatred reached out like a hand toward her enemy. She was too angry to cry. Crying was a warm thing. Sara was cold inside. Cold and hard.

Though she was hobbling badly, Lady Drume did not ask for help. Sara did not offer it.

In the cabin, Lady Drume turned and said, "Get ready for lunch, Sara."

"I don't want lunch."

"Don't be silly. Of course you want lunch."

"No I don't. I feel sick."

"You are simply being sullen. I dislike sullen children. You cannot possibly be sick. The sea is very calm today."

"I feel sick."

Lady Drume snorted.

"Very well. If you choose to sulk in here, you may do so. I am going to lunch. Meanwhile, I suggest you give some thought to your selfish behavior this morning."

Lady Drume hobbled out.

Sara climbed onto her bunk and lay still, staring at the ceiling. The bristles on the back of her neck itched, reminding her of how short her hair was. The barber had tapered it just like a boy's. It ended at her ears. At the front, it covered her whole forehead, down to her eyebrows. Her eyebrows probably didn't even show. She was ugly. She would never look in a mirror again. She would never leave this cabin again. Ugly.

Her mother's voice echoed in her memory. "Remember the nightingale when things are not going well," she had said. Sara tried to be brave like the nightingale, but it was no good. All she could think of was that nightingales were graceful, lovely creatures. And she was ugly.

Sara turned to the wall and lay rigid. The ship rocked her gently, but it brought her no comfort.

Footsteps approached and stopped outside the cabin door. There was a knock. She did not answer.

"Sara?"

She could not speak.

"Sara? May I come in?" Dr. Wetherill's voice was anxious.

"Yes." Her voice was scratchy. Her throat was tight and aching. She covered her head with her arms.

Dr. Wetherill came to the side of the bunk.

"Lady Drume told me you didn't feel like lunch. I thought I'd see if I could help."

He paused. Sara felt him staring at her. After a short silence, he gently pulled her arms away from her head.

"Oh, Sara!" he said. "Oh, my dear. Oh, Sara!"

The warm sympathy in his voice melted the ice in Sara's heart. Turning to him, she wept on his shoulder as though she would never stop. Gasping, hiccuping, all the pain poured out—pain for her lost hair—and her mother so far away—for Domino left behind—and her father fighting in the sky over distant England.

"There, there," murmured Dr. Wetherill, holding her close. "There, there," he said, patting her back gently. "There, there."

It took a long time for her sobbing to stop. At last, there were no tears left. Empty and exhausted, she lay against his shoulder, and still he held her. In the silence, the ship rocked her. Her eyelids drooped.

Dr. Wetherill put her back gently on her pillow. "I want you to rest now. I'll be back in an hour's time. Sleep now."

As the cabin door closed softly behind him, Sara slept . . .

Echoing voices sounded faintly from far away, calling. She was at the bottom of a deep, dark well.

"Sara . . . Sara . . ."

The voices got louder, more urgent, and suddenly Sara was awake. There was a knock at the cabin door and Dr. Wetherill's voice, calling, "Wake up, Sara! It's time to get up now!"

He came in, followed by Maggie and Ernie.

"We've come to take you to lunch," he said, cheerfully. "Up you get! Run in and wash the sleep out of your eyes and then we'll be off."

Sara climbed groggily down the ladder. As she turned, she caught the startled look which Maggie was not quick enough to hide, and she remembered. Clapping her hand to her head, she ran for the bathroom to hide.

Maggie followed her in, saying, "Give me your comb, Sara. I'll fix it nice. I'm ever so good with 'air. Everybody says so."

As the door closed behind them, Sara heard Ernie say to Dr. Wetherill, "There oughter be

114

a law against wot that old girl's done to Sara!"

Maggie took the comb and Sara stood still, staring at herself in the mirror. Maggie set to work and combed it smooth. Then, taking part of the fringe that hung limply to Sara's eyebrows, she drew it back to one side, anchoring it with a little clip. On the other side, she tucked the short hair neatly behind Sara's ear.

"There!" she said. "That's better!"

"Thank you, Maggie," Sara whispered.

"Come on then! We're going to 'ave a beano!"

"A what?"

"You'll find out!"

Dr. Wetherill and Ernie were waiting. Ernie nodded approvingly. "Come on, love!" he said, linking his arm with hers. Maggie placed herself on the other side and, together, the three friends and Dr. Wetherill set off through the ship.

There was no sign of Lady Drume. Anyway, Sara did not care where she was. If Lady Drume could not find her when she came back to the cabin, maybe she would think Sara had jumped overboard and feel guilty for the rest of her life. Maybe she would jump off the ship herself in a fit of remorse. Sara hoped she would.

Dr. Wetherill led the way. They went along

the promenade deck, past Lady Drume's empty deck chair, down the iron steps to A Deck below, then down some more steps to B Deck. They went through a door and along a passage and then downwards again.

"This must be C Deck," Sara said.

"Yes," said Ernie, "we sleep along there."

"Where are we going?"

"You'll see!" said Ernie. They went down some more stairs.

It was noisy in this corridor. Machinery chugged nearby, so loud that Sara's body throbbed in time with it.

"Engine room!" yelled Dr. Wetherill, cupping his hand to his mouth to make himself heard.

"I know. This is where I got my nosebleed," Sara yelled back.

They went on and descended another level.

We must be a long way underwater by now, Sara thought.

At last, just ahead of them, they heard the clatter of dishes, accompanied by a voice, singing loudly. They came to a large kitchen. Sparky was waiting in the doorway.

"There you are!" he greeted them. "Just in time. We're all ready. Wait till you see the surprise old Taffy has got for you, Miss Sara!"

A wizened little dark-eyed man in a white

apron and chef's hat came forward. He welcomed them in a voice like an organ.

"Come in, come in! Welcome to Taffy's kitchen!"

"Where are we?" asked Sara, as she let herself be pulled along by the cook.

"This is what we call the crew's mess," replied Taffy. "The passengers' food is prepared in the passengers' galley. But the crew has its meals down here, and we have our own kind of food—none of that fancy stuff they want up there. Just good plain food that sticks to the ribs for a while!"

A long table stood at one end of the kitchen and seven places were set on the white tablecloth.

"Sit down, all!" cried Taffy.

They sat around the table like a family, smiling at each other in anticipation. Sara was hungry. It was long past lunchtime. Taffy set some dishes down on the table and then, seating himself at the head of the table, uncovered them.

"O-o-h!" breathed Sara.

Two dozen plump sausages lay side by side, gleaming gold and brown, in the pewter dish. They smelled better than any sausages had ever smelled before.

She looked up to find everyone grinning at

her, and she realized everyone had known about Taffy's surprise but her.

"How did you know?" Sara asked in astonishment. "How could you know this was my favorite thing to eat in the whole world?"

As she spoke, someone dashed into the kitchen and flung himself into the seventh chair.

"Whew!" he exclaimed. "I thought they'd never stop eating up there! I was sure I'd miss the party."

"Mr. Hornby!" cried Sara. "You told them, Mr. Hornby!"

"I cannot tell a lie, miss," grinned Hornby. "When old Sparky here asked me what you liked to eat best in the world, I had no trouble at all in telling him!"

They all laughed and then settled down to their meal. Sara ate slowly, savoring every juicy mouthful. She wanted it to last as long as possible. These were her friends and she loved them.

THIRTEEN

Bird's Eye View

"What shall we do now?"

Sara looked at Maggie and Ernie. The three friends were standing together near the deck rail. The sea sparkled below them in the afternoon sun and a soft breeze lightly lifted Sara's short hair. It felt like her mother's touch.

"Won't the old girl be on the lookout for you?" asked Ernie.

"I don't care if she is!" answered Sara. "I hope she searches all over the ship for me, until her stupid old ankle swells up like an elephant's. I hope her whole body swells up, all over, till she looks like a . . . like a barrage balloon!"

Maggie and Ernie laughed.

"Can't you just see old Lady Drume floating in the sky over London with all the other barrage balloons?" asked Sara, giggling.

"If the Jerries caught sight of 'er, they'd fly straight back to Berlin!" exclaimed Ernie.

"Come on," Sara said, impatiently. She felt wild and free. "I'll race you both around the deck!"

"You're on!" Ernie said.

"Ready, steady, go!" shouted Sara.

She fled away ahead of them along the deck, glimpsing startled faces as she zigzagged through the passengers, strolling after their lunch. She felt laughter welling up inside her, as she headed at a dead run around the corner, scattering a little group of people against the deck rail. She didn't care. Ahead of her she spotted George and Rosie. She saw their heads swing around and their mouths gape open as she tore by.

Glancing over her shoulder, Sara saw Ernie pounding after her. Behind him came Maggie. Sara quickened her pace. Three minutes later, puffing and panting, they were all back where they had started from.

"Whew! I beat you!" laughed Sara.

"Yes . . . well . . . next time, I'll try 'arder," said Ernie. "I could of beat you if I'd been really trying!"

"You could not, Ernie Barker!" his sister said. "You was running your 'ardest and you know it!"

"Well . . . it was close, anyway," Sara said.

Just as she spoke, they heard Lady Drume further along the deck.

"The girl must be found!" she boomed. "I simply will not tolerate such behavior! She seems to have taken completely the wrong attitude toward this whole matter. After all, what was done was entirely for her own good!"

"It was not!" muttered Sara. "It was because I forgot about you and your silly book. You did it to get back at me!"

In the distance, Lady Drume came around the corner, leaning heavily on the arm of the bishop.

"We'd better 'op it," Ernie said.

"I know where to go," whispered Sara. "Follow me!"

She turned and ran away from Lady Drume toward the hospital.

"You can't hide in the 'ospital," Maggie said. "That's the first place she'll look. She knows you and the doctor are chums."

"We're not *going* to the hospital," said Sara, her eyes bright. "We're going up *there!*"

Maggie and Ernie looked upward.

Ernie began to grin.

"Someone will see us!" gasped Maggie.

"No they won't—not if we're quick," answered Sara. "You first, Ernie."

She heard Lady Drume's lopsided step approaching.

"Hurry up!" she whispered.

Ernie went up the steel beam like a monkey.

"You're next, Maggie," Sara said. "Go on—hurry up before she comes!"

"Oo-er! I don't know if I can."

"Yes, you can. Hurry!" urged Sara. "I'll be right behind you."

Maggie climbed slowly, slipping and sliding awkwardly. With Sara giving her a push from below, she got to the top of the beam finally and dropped out of sight into the lifeboat. Glancing down the deck, Sara could see Lady Drume rounding the corner.

"Get a move on!" breathed Ernie from above.

"Here I come!" said Sara.

She scrambled up the beam, clutching with her fingers, slipping backwards so that the metal burned her hands as she slid, catching hold again with muscles that throbbed with the strain, curling her toes to get a better grip. Looking down for a moment, she saw the sea swirling far below at the side of the ship. A swimmy, dizzy feeling swept over her and she jerked her head upwards frantically. She inched on her way, clinging to the beam, until at last she grabbed the wooden gunwhale of the boat. Grunting with the effort, she hauled herself over and dropped in. She lay still, her heart pumping.

"Did she see you?" Maggie asked.

"I don't know. Ssh!"

They lay together in the bottom of Number Sixteen, holding their breath. The enemy's footsteps clumped along the deck.

". . . can't imagine . . . extraordinary . . . where she's disappeared to . . ." The pair below proceeded slowly out of hearing distance.

The children lay side by side on their stomachs, their hearts beating in their throats.

"Is it safe to look out?" whispered Sara.

"I'll have a dekko and let you know," answered Ernie. Carefully, so as not to rock the boat and give them away, he edged up to the side, raised the canvas cover a fraction of an inch, and peeked out.

"All clear!" he breathed, and the girls knelt up to join him.

They soon realized that the deck below their hideout was a busy highway. Dr. Wetherill hurried by with his bag. The lady pianist fluttered along, on the arm of a very old gentleman with a pointed beard. Rosie ran by. "I can't find them anywhere!" she yelled. "Arthur, see if they're in the library." Ernie grinned at Sara. They heard more footsteps. It was Mr. Hobbs, and for a moment, to their horror, he cast a glance upward at Number Sixteen. They ducked their heads and waited. The wooden ribs in the bottom of the lifeboat dug into Sara's knees and the beating of her heart almost hurt. At last, unable to wait any longer, she crawled back up till just her eyes looked out. The deck was empty. Mr. Hobbs had gone. She lay down again to rest her knees.

"Hey, you three!"

Their eyes widened as a loud whisper came from below. Carefully, they looked out. Sparky was standing underneath the boat, pretending to look out to sea.

"'Ow did you know we was up 'ere?" demanded Ernie.

"You won't tell?" Maggie begged.

Sparky looked insulted. "Me squeal on my mates?" he said. "What do you take me for! I'm on watch on the bridge and I spotted you from up there. Having fun?"

"Oh, yes!" answered Sara.

"Good. Be careful, though. Don't slip when you come down. Got to go. I could only get away for a minute. Cheerio!"

"Bye."

The children relaxed again. Ernie and Maggie were content to lie on their backs, listening to the hiss of the sea below them. But Sara could not bear to leave her watching post for more than a minute.

It gives you a whole different feeling about things, she thought. The people going about their business below were like people on a stage. Like the actors she had seen in the theater the year before. She felt apart from them. And, though Maggie and Ernie were there beside her, she felt apart from them, too. She felt alone, suspended like a star between sky and sea.

Sara wondered if everyone had these "alone" feelings every now and then. She'd never asked. It might have to do with not being part of a big, noisy family. Even when she went to stay with her cousins, whom she'd known all her life, there would sometimes come a moment—right in the middle of doing things—when she felt . . . separate. She had once heard her father say, "Sara is a bit awkward among the other children. She ought to mix in with them more." Her mother had answered, "Don't worry about her, dear. She's just a bit shy. She's alone so much."

Sara didn't mind being alone. Alone meant

making up stories and watching the clouds and talking out loud to Domino, without someone thinking you were funny. Alone was not the same as lonely.

A motion far below interrupted her dreaming . . . a silvery movement in the water that streamed away from the bow. A few moments passed and then, abruptly, joyously, a great fish arched out of the water, followed closely by another, then a third and a fourth. No! Not fish. Dolphins! Keeping perfect time with the big ship, the dolphins danced along beside it. They didn't seem the least bit afraid.

Sara watched them, unwilling to take her eyes away for a moment in case they vanished. Ernie and Maggie lay unaware in the bottom of the boat. She didn't want to tell them about the dolphins. They were hers. Hadn't they waited until she was alone before surfacing? She gazed on, entranced. But, after a few moments, she began to feel ashamed of not sharing them with her friends.

"Maggie . . . Ernie . . . come and look!" she whispered.

Taking their cue from her hushed voice, the others crept to the side and looked over.

"Ooh!" Ernie sucked in his breath. "Cor! I never seen a fish the size of them there—not even in Billingsgate Market!"

Maggie didn't say a word. But her eyes shone.

The children were silent for a long time. They watched the dolphins and the dolphins seemed to watch them, saluting them with round, bright eyes and cheerful smiles, each time they broke from the water.

Finally, Ernie said, "I'm 'ungry. It must be near dinnertime. We'll have to be going, Sara."

Maggie added, "It must be late. I've got a dreadful 'eadache and I always gets an 'eadache when I'm 'ungry."

Sara nodded glumly. She was going to have to face Lady Drume.

"All right," she said.

Choosing a safe moment, they slid down the beam to the deck.

"See you later," Ernie said. He and his sister ran off.

Sara walked slowly toward Cabin 110.

She could hear a man's voice inside.

". . . sure nothing can have happened to her, Lady Drume. I have several of the crew looking. She'll turn up. You know children!"

"That's just it!" replied Lady Drume. "I don't know children, not the way I used to. Not any more. They aren't the same. My own children grew up in a different world. I cannot be sure of things any more."

Sara paused in the narrow corridor. Children! Lady Drume had had children of her own? Sara could not imagine her as a mother. Lady Drume had mentioned Admiral Drume, but Sara had thought of him as a statue on a pedestal, not as someone's father.

Lady Drume continued. "I . . . I'm . . . afraid I did something which upset her this morning. Of course you never know how someone else's child is going to react. That's why I'm more than ordinarily worried about her."

Good! thought Sara. It's *good* she's been worried. Serves her right! And I'm glad she's sorry about cutting my hair. But being sorry won't bring it back. I wish I could hide from her for ever and ever!

But Sara knew she could not hide forever. Taking a deep breath, she pushed open the door and went in.

"Sara!" cried Lady Drume, turning a strained face toward her. "Dear child, where have you been?"

The purser rose from his chair. "There you are, Lady Drume. What did I tell you? I said she'd turn up. Well, I must be off. Things to do!" He left the cabin.

"Sara, how could you worry me so much,

you naughty girl!" Lady Drume's voice began rising to its usual strength. But then she caught herself, and continued more quietly. "Where have you been? Nobody knew where you were. I was afraid something had happened to you."

"Oh, I'm so sorry, Lady Drume," replied Sara, in a cool, high voice. "I didn't think you would be worrying about *me*. I was just around and about . . ." She paused and then, looking Lady Drume in the eye, went on, ". . . with my friends, Maggie and Ernie."

"I might have known it!" Lady Drume's face darkened. "They are nothing but a bad influence on you. If I had my way . . ." Her voice began rising again. She broke off with an obvious effort, and took a deep breath. "Well, well. Ha, ha. We must get ready for dinner, Sara. Come here, and I will tidy your hair. It looks quite nice tucked back that way."

"Maggie combed it like that for me," Sara said.

"I see . . . well . . . she, ah, seems to know something about hair. Her mother is probably a hairdresser of some sort."

"Her mother is a cook in the dockworkers' canteen," Sara replied.

Lady Drume's lips tightened. "I see." Her

square, freckled hands brushed Sara's hair briskly in a no-nonsense way. "Ah . . . Sara . . . ah . . . the haircut we gave you this morning will be good for your hair, you know. Thicken it . . ." She gave Sara's hair a final pat, unexpectedly gentle. "There. Well. It is a long time since I brushed a child's hair. I am afraid I am rather out of practice. Ha, ha."

Lady Drume was being very friendly. Sara knew it was an apology of a sort.

"Do you and the Admiral have children?" she asked.

"Two. We . . . I . . . have two. They are quite grown up by this time, though. Our son, William, is in the Navy, of course. Stationed in Malta at present, I believe, though naturally, he is not permitted to be exact as to his where-abouts."

"And the other one?"

"We have a daughter—Pamela. She is married and lives in Victoria, British Columbia."

"Oh," said Sara. "Then you'll be able to see her when we get to Vancouver."

"Yes. They have just had a baby son. Named him Robert Algernon, after . . ." Lady Drume's voice roughened. "How the Admiral would have loved to see his first grandchild!"

"The Admiral?" said Sara. She felt Lady

Drume was waiting for her to ask about him.

"Gone, Sara. Gone. They asked him to come out of retirement when the war began. He knew his duty to his country and off he went. They hadn't been at sea more than two months before his vessel was sunk with all hands."

"Oh," whispered Sara, horrified. After a moment, she said, "I'm sorry I worried you today, Lady Drume."

"Well, well. Enough of all this." Lady Drume patted her shoulder. "We must be off to dinner. Come along, child."

They walked down the corridor together.

FOURTEEN
Fogbank

Sara woke the next morning and leaned down from her bunk to look out of the porthole. Still the sea, the same gray sea, tumbling and rolling as far as the horizon. For a moment, it seemed they had not moved since the previous morning, or the morning before that—that the U-boat attack—and her hair being cut off—and the feast with her friends—and the dolphins—had all come and gone while the Duke of Perth lay motionless in the same spot in the ocean. But for the faint vibration of the ship's engines humming through her bunk, she could have believed it.

What about her mother and father, thousands of miles away by now? Was there a raid going on this minute? Was Domino crouched trembling in the garden shelter? What was *happening* to them?

Sara lay back and stared at the ceiling. Her mother and father were living a different life now—a life without her. They would be thinking of nothing but the war and how to get through each day to the next. While she was stuck out here in the ocean, leaving the sights and sounds of war, and her family, far, far behind.

Last day on board, she thought. By this time tomorrow, they would be docked in Montreal and she would begin her life in a new country. Canada. What would it be like? All she knew was that it was big. She'd seen that much on the map her father had shown her. As big as the Atlantic Ocean, which was taking four days and five nights to cross.

Sara's stomach grumbled. It was time to get up and go to breakfast. While she was dressing, she planned her day.

She and Maggie and Ernie would pick their time carefully and then, when nobody was looking, they would climb up into Number Sixteen again. They would watch the dolphins and, probably, from up there, they would be the first people on the whole ship to sight Canada. But before Sara went off to do *anything*, she would be sure to tell Lady Drume not to worry about her. Lady Drume had had a very sad thing happen to her. Sara had made up her mind to give Lady Drume no further trouble.

But Maggie and Ernie were not at their table. None of them was in the dining-room . . .

Sara ate quickly, anxious to get up on deck.

"May I go for a walk, Lady Drume?" she asked.

"Very well, my dear. Be careful," Lady Drume answered. "I shall spend an hour reading in the cabin, and then I will come up and join you for some exercise. My foot is feeling much better today."

Sara skipped out on deck, looking for the children. Arthur came around the corner. "Where are the others?" he asked.

"I don't know. I'm looking for them, too," said Sara.

"I'll look on B Deck," said Arthur.

Far out on the horizon, there was a bank of fog resting pale above the water. Sara stopped to gaze at it, thinking how solid it looked, and wondering why it was there.

Sparky came up behind her. "Should sight Cape Race before long, miss." He nodded at the fog in the distance. "Always get fog around Newfoundland."

"Newfoundland?" She thought of the map.

"Newfoundland's in Canada! I mean . . . it's near Canada, isn't it? Are we nearly there?"

"Tomorrow morning, before you wake up, we'll be there."

Sara stared at the fog, which hung between the sky and the sea like a ghostly barrier. "Is it *always* there?" she asked, fascinated. There was something menacing about it.

"Just about always," answered Sparky. "It's where the warm Gulf Stream water coming up from the south hits the cold Labrador current coming down from the north. When those two mix together, that just naturally makes for a lot of fog. A lot of fish, too. These waters beneath us are alive with them." He smiled. "The fish are having a holiday these days! Not many fishermen are going to risk coming out after them, with the German U-boats lurking about!"

Sara thought of the dolphins. She wouldn't worry about finding anyone. She would go and watch the dolphins for a while, by herself.

Waving goodbye to Sparky, she headed for the bow, remembering that he had said long ago that it was the best place to watch from. Long ago . . . why, it was really only three days ago. But it seemed much longer. The new world was just a day away.

Sara came out on the foredeck and, wiggling under some safety ropes, she wedged herself right into the angle of the ship's bow. Looking down, far down, she could see the sharp, clean line of the bow of the ship cleaving the water with a cheerful hiss, hiss, hiss. The gray water curled up into a creamy froth on either side. Sara peered down eagerly, first on one side, then on the other, waiting for the dolphins to break out of the foam and arch upward in greeting. Minutes passed before she realized they were gone.

She didn't want to believe it at first.

Perhaps they've gone for a little swim, she thought. I'll just wait here a bit longer. They'll probably see me up here and come back.

She stretched out on a flat shelf that jutted inwards from the ship's side, and waited. Every now and then, she got up and looked downwards. But the dolphins did not return. She knew it was silly to feel sad about it, but she did.

After one last look down into the empty foam, she turned and left the bow. Walking slowly back along the deck, she glanced ahead and saw Number Sixteen hanging in its cradle. A thought struck her. I'll climb up into Number Sixteen. Maybe from up there I'll be able to see the dolphins. They might only be a little way away.

When she got there, she looked carefully to left and right and then, seeing nobody in either direction, hauled herself up the beam toward the lifeboat. It was easier doing it for the second time. But, at the top, she found that her fingers were not strong enough to unhook the canvas cover. She curled her legs hard around the beam and, clinging with one arm, struggled with her other hand to release it. But she could not overcome the tension that held the hook fast.

Bother! I can't do it alone. I need Maggie and Ernie, she said to herself. She slid backwards down the beam. It's no use waiting for Arthur. I'll have to find them myself.

Sara headed for their dormitory. Passenger Lounge C, Maggie had said. But when she got there, the lounge was empty. No cots. No suitcases. No children.

Maybe I'm on the wrong deck, thought Sara. Backing up, she checked the number of the lounge. "Passenger Lounge C," it read.

Sara ran along the passageway until she found a sailor polishing some brass railings.

"Where is everybody?" she asked him.

"Who, miss?"

"My friends."

"Oh. I believe they've been taken off the ship, miss."

"Taken off the ship? What do you mean? All of them? What for?"

"I don't know, miss. Maybe they've been misbehaving themselves!" replied the sailor, with a grin.

Sara looked wildly up and down the corridor.

"You're joking! Don't make fun of me! Where are they? They can't *really* be gone! How could they be taken off the ship in the middle of the ocean?"

"Well, miss," the sailor said, seriously. "Technically, it *is* possible. We're standing off Newfoundland just now and so, if necessary, they could be taken there by the Coast Guard. I'm only telling you what I heard. When I came on duty, my mate told me that the lot from Lounge C were going to be taken off the ship. But he didn't say why. Of course, they might still be on board, miss. It wasn't that long ago. Try the promenade deck, near the purser's office. If you hurry, maybe you'll catch up with them."

Sara turned and ran down the passageway.

"Good luck, miss. Hope you find them!" the sailor called after her.

Sara ran through the inner corridors and up the stairways until she came out on the promenade deck. With a lift of her heart, she could see, far at the other end, a line of children waiting by the ship's railing. Each one carried a suitcase. Mrs. Bourne, her head still in bandages, had two children by the hand.

Sara ran toward them, her heart pounding, her mouth dry. But halfway along the deck, a barrier had been put up and an officer stood on guard next to it.

What could have happened?

"Now then, miss," said the officer, barring the way like a policeman. "You cannot come past here. You can see the barrier, can't you."

"But I want to talk to my friends!" Sara cried.

"Sorry, miss. Nobody is allowed by. Captain's orders. You're not supposed to go near them. They are being taken off the ship, miss."

"I know! But, please! I've got to! They're my friends. I must see them. I . . . want to . . . I have . . . to . . . to say goodbye!"

Lady Drume's voice sounded behind her.

"Don't argue, Sara. You may not go past. You heard what this officer said."

"But, Lady Drume! They are taking my friends off the ship. All the children from Lounge C." Sara clutched Lady Drume's arm.

"You can stop it, Lady Drume! Please stop it! What have they done? They can't have done anything bad enough to be put off the ship!"

"They haven't done anything, Sara. It is simply that they have all broken out with the measles. At least, most of them have, and the others will be sure to get them in the next day or two. Must have contracted them at the evacuation center in Billingsgate. Captain Moulderby-Jones and Dr. Wetherill and I discussed the situation after breakfast." Lady Drume smiled. "As was natural, they came to me for my advice, knowing of my wide hospital experience." She drew herself up grandly. "I advised them that it would be best for Dr. Wetherill to take the infected children to the isolation ward in a Newfoundland hospital, so as to avoid starting an epidemic of measles at the evacuee center in Toronto to say nothing of on board this ship!"

While Lady Drume was speaking, Sara craned over the ship's railing. A Coast Guard cutter was moored beside the Duke of Perth's ladder, which hung down over the side.

"But, Lady Drume!" she protested. "You knew Maggie and Ernie were my special friends. I didn't even get a chance to see them.

They'll think I didn't even care enough to come and say goodbye!"

"Well, as to that, Sara, I must say I am delighted you did *not* see them. I think you will agree with me now that it is a good thing I prevented you from having much to do with them."

"But couldn't they stay on board?" Sara pleaded. "You could arrange it. I know you could. You can do anything, Lady Drume. The Captain would do what you want."

"He is doing *precisely* what I want, Sara. This is by far the best way to handle the situation. Speaking for myself, possibly due to my rather sheltered upbringing, I have never had the measles. And I understand that measles in adulthood are nothing to trifle with!"

Sara's eyes brimmed with angry tears as she leaned over the railing. The children were climbing slowly down the ship's ladder into the Coast Guard cutter. Finally they were all aboard. She could see Dr. Wetherill sitting in the stern with the smallest child on his lap. The ship's ladder was pulled back aboard the Duke of Perth. Sara stared downward, searching for her friends' faces among the others far below.

The cutter's engines roared, the water

141

churned about the spinning propeller at the stern of the boat, and it began pulling away, heading toward the fog-hidden shore of Newfoundland.

Sara waved frantically, making huge circles with her arms. She saw two of the heads below turn upwards. "They're looking for me!" she cried.

Ernie grinned and pointed, then Maggie turned to scan the railing.

Sara waved and waved and, as the cutter was swallowed up by the fog, the last thing she saw was Ernie with his fingers raised high in a V-for-Victory salute. Then they were gone. Vanished from her life, as surely as the dolphins.

FIFTEEN
Goodbyes

Cabin 110 was bare—their bags had been packed and taken away. As Sara followed Lady Drume to the dining room, the ship felt dead beneath her feet. Somehow it reflected her own mood, now that they had finally arrived. Why did she feel so empty, so quiet inside, instead of being excited and curious about her new country? Instead, it seemed as though the feeling part of her had been swallowed up by the fog.

Sara could not forgive Lady Drume for having Ernie and Maggie taken off the ship. All the previous day, she had tramped around the deck angrily. How could she ever have felt sorry for her?

At breakfast, Lady Drume polished off a large helping of eggs and bacon and then moved around the dining room importantly,

143

stopping at the tables to say goodbye to the people she had met on the voyage.

Sara had said goodbye to Sparky the day before, as the ship steamed quietly into the St. Lawrence Estuary under an applegreen evening sky. There was nobody else she wanted to see. She ate her breakfast slowly, without tasting any of it.

An hour later she stood waiting in the main lounge. The children headed for the evacuee center had been lined up against the wall while the ladies looking after them ran about checking their lists. She could see Donald and George wrestling near the door. Rosie wasn't there. She'd been sent away with Maggie and Ernie.

Sara shifted nervously from one foot to the other. She was standing in a different line and Lady Drume had left her to go across the room. Sara could see her shaking hands with the bishop.

"Hi, honey!"

Sara jumped. It was her turn. She was face to face with the immigration officer—her first Canadian.

"Hi, honey!" he said again. "Welcome to Canada! You're going to like it here with us."

"Yes," Sara answered.

She felt anchored there in front of him, weighted to the spot by her blue wool coat which dragged heavily on her shoulders. She pushed a wisp of hair impatiently out of her eye, but it flopped right back again.

The Canadian officer looked down at the sheaf of papers by his hand. He flipped through the pages of her passport.

"Hey! Wait a minute!" he exclaimed suddenly. "I don't think you *are* Sara Warren!" He frowned up at her. "This passport picture looks like a different young lady to me!"

Sara stared down at the picture. A smiling girl with smooth, shining hair arranged on either side of her head looked up at her. The man was right. She did not look like that Sara Warren at all. She had tried to fix her cropped hair neatly that morning, the way Maggie had done. But it hung around her face in a forlorn mop. Her heart thudded with fear. She was going to be arrested and flung in prison for pretending to be someone she was not. Her chin trembled.

"I . . . I . . ." she stammered.

The officer looked up from his papers again, smiling. Then he jumped up in concern.

"Oh, honey!" he exclaimed. "I was just fooling! I was just joshing you a bit, because I noticed you'd had your hair cut since your passport picture was taken. I didn't mean anything by it—I was just having a bit of fun!" He patted her shoulder awkwardly. "Why, you're as welcome as the flowers in May, Sara Warren! Now then. Where's my stamp?" He searched his cluttered table. "There!" he said, stamping her passport. "You're officially admitted to the Dominion of Canada! Now—let's see a smile on that pretty face!"

Sara's thudding heart gradually calmed and she stood there, drained of feeling. Fear, excitement, happiness, misery. She felt nothing.

Lady Drume pushed her way back to Sara's side through the crowd.

"Finished? Good! Now, we must hurry, Sara. No dawdling and mooning about, please! The Vancouver train leaves in half an hour."

SIXTEEN

Tracks

The train hurtled along, swaying slightly. Sara sat at lunch in the dining car, listening to the jingling of the glasses and cutlery. Lady Drume, sitting opposite, was working her way through a large plateful of food. Sara prodded a piece of meat around her plate, but she could not force herself to put it in her mouth.

She put her fork down and, leaning her chin on her hand, she stared out of the window at the dun-colored prairie rolling by outside. First Manitoba, then Saskatchewan, now Alberta. The umber plain that had been rushing past her window hour after hour after endless hour was vast and flat and featureless. Only an occasional farmhouse, stuck out in the middle of nowhere beside a windbreak of raggedy trees, broke the monotony.

During the three days and nights since they

had left Montreal, Sara had learned to walk through the swaying train without losing her balance. She liked going up and down the length of it, looking at the people.

But most of all, she liked the moment every night when the porter swung her bunk down out of the ceiling. She loved the idea that people could walk along the aisle of the train, all unknowing that she lay hidden in her night-clothes on the other side of the swinging green curtain which screened her bunk. She had felt the same that afternoon up in Number Sixteen. With one difference . . . here she was alone. And, this time, she was lonely. There was no Ernie or Maggie beside her to share the suspense and the fun.

During the daylight hours, Lady Drume scribbled busily on a pad in her leather writing case.

"Would you like to play Snap, Lady Drume?" asked Sara, shuffling the cards the porter had given her.

"No, Sara. I dislike card games. And I must attend to my correspondence," replied Lady Drume, without looking up. "Read your book."

Sara had sighed and laid out the cards for another game of Patience.

I know, she thought. I'll write to Maggie and

Ernie! But in the same moment, she remembered she had never got the address of the children's center from Maggie. None of them had ever talked of the time when they would have to say goodbye. Somehow it had seemed as though, if they didn't say anything out loud, then in some magic way it would never happen.

As the dreary days ground by, Sara settled into a pattern of reading, followed by staring out of the window, followed by more reading. For a day and a half, she had had a bad headache.

Lady Drume's voice trumpeted over her thoughts, and she wrenched her gaze away from the window.

"You look droopy!"

Sara flushed, as the other diners turned to inspect the droopy one.

"You are picking at your food again, Sara! It is not proper for you to leave your food when there are children starving all over the world. Look at me! Do you ever see me leave anything on *my* plate?"

Sara sighed. She could never see the connection between her own poor eating habits and the starving children elsewhere in the world.

"I'm just not hungry, that's all," Sara replied. She didn't want to tell Lady Drume about her aching head and her sore throat, and the heavy, hot, prickly feeling all over her body.

"The trouble is, you are not getting enough fresh air and exercise," Lady Drume said. "Never mind. Tomorrow morning we arrive in Vancouver and you'll feel better in no time! Good gracious!" She pointed out the window. "Look ahead there! Mountains!"

Sara's eyes widened. She had never seen mountains. Searching the horizon, she could just make out far ahead a blue line of mountains which marked the end of the prairie.

A phrase she had once heard in church popped into Sara's head.

"It looks like the promised land!" she breathed.

"It does indeed!" nodded Lady Drume. "A very apt description, child."

By dinnertime, they were climbing steadily up through the mountain passes and, just before bedtime, the train slowed down, the tolling of its big bell echoing against the mountainsides. Its great brakes hissed and screeched as it drew to a stop at a small station. Everybody poured out of the train.

"Breathe deeply, Sara!" Lady Drume commanded. "This is good air! Fill your lungs with it!"

Sara did not need to be told. She raised her hot face thirstily to the cool air.

The sky, which had seemed so vast out on the prairie, here was just a circle over their heads. Mountains rose all around them, their sides in deepening shadow. Their high peaks were touched with rose and gold, as the sun set beyond them. Sara gazed upward and glimpsed the pure shine of snow. Snow in summertime!

The next morning, the long trans-Canada train wound at last into Vancouver, more than three thousand miles of forest and prairie and mountains behind it. It slowed on the curved track, its bell clanging, and stopped with a shuddering hiss of its brakes.

The passengers gathered their belongings together and got ready to leave the train. Sara had a hollow, giddy feeling in her stomach. In the next few minutes, she would meet her Uncle Duncan and Aunt Jean and begin her new life with them. At long last, she would be able to say goodbye to Lady Drume, who had become more and more irritable with every day on the train. But . . . supposing her unknown relatives did not like her? Or . . . sup-

151

posing she did not like them? Supposing she hated living in Canada?

Her father's words echoed in her mind—"In wartime, we must all do things we don't want to do. That's why you have to leave here and go to Canada."

Sara swallowed hard as she headed up the aisle of the train behind Lady Drume. Her throat hurt and her body prickled under her scratchy coat.

Lady Drume glanced over her shoulder. "I must say I shall be delighted to get off this stuffy train!" she announced. "I have a most frightful headache!"

"Me too," Sara replied.

Lady Drume looked sharply at her.

"Lack of fresh air and exercise! Not healthy being cooped up in a train for days on end!"

Standing on the platform, Sara looked around bewildered at the crowd of people waiting. I don't know what Uncle Duncan looks like, she thought. How will he know what I look like?

The bright sun hurt her eyes and she blinked painfully. Her whole body seemed to be rolling, as though she was still walking the decks of H.M.S. Duke of Perth.

"There's our Sara! I'd know her anywhere!

The image of her beautiful mother!" called out a cheerful voice. The next moment, Sara was swooped up by a big man in a tweed jacket with leather patches on its elbows. He smelled of pipe tobacco, just like her own father. A feeling of relief overwhelmed her.

With his arm securely around Sara's shoulder, Uncle Duncan shook hands with Lady Drume, while Aunt Jean, a small, plump woman, smiled and took Sara's hand firmly in her own.

"We are so happy you have come, Sara. With our own Mary off at school so much of the time, I've missed having a little girl around the house. We think ourselves very lucky that your folks will lend you to us for a while!"

Next to them, Lady Drume's voice rose in volume. ". . . perfectly dreadful, Mr. McLeod. Food was abominable on the train. Couldn't eat a thing!" She went on, "I plan to relax briefly at my daughter's home in Victoria, while coordinating the local war relief drive. And then it's back to the front again! My country needs me!"

Lady Drume's chin lifted proudly. But, as she spoke, her strong voice trembled in an unfamiliar way. Sara looked up at her curiously. Her face appeared more than usually flushed, and there was a faint dew of perspiration along her upper lip. She passed her large, square hand across her forehead, where it was shadowed by the brim of her hat.

"Warm day!" she remarked. "Reminds me of the tropics." She squared her shoulders under her brown cape. "Well. Sara is in good hands, and I must soldier on. I understand that the ferry to Victoria leaves on the hour."

The moment Sara had been waiting for had finally come. It was time to say goodbye to Lady Drume. They looked at each other, trying to find the right words.

Lady Drume spoke first. "I am afraid you and I have sometimes misunderstood one another, my dear. But I did my best to look after you and deliver you safely to your destination." She patted Sara's cheek. "Be happy, Sara. And . . . and . . . don't forget all about England, now that you are going to live in a new land."

Sara looked up at her old enemy.

"Goodbye, Lady Drume," she said, "and . . . thank you for bringing me here, and . . . and . . ."

Sara's voice faltered and, suddenly, to her own astonishment, she found herself stepping forward and hugging Lady Drume hard around her ironclad waist.

"Oh! My! My!" murmured Lady Drume. "Goodness gracious me, child!" and slowly, gracefully, her tweed cape billowing about her like a deflating parachute, she sank unconscious to the platform.

SEVENTEEN
Fever

For a moment, everybody stared at Lady Drume without moving. She lay like a beached whale in the bright sunshine.

Then Sara burst out, "What did I do to her? I just hugged her! I didn't mean to do anything bad!" She stared down at Lady Drume, who lay at her feet, her eyes closed, a puzzled frown on her face. The flush had faded from her cheeks, leaving a chalky pallor, mottled with harsh red splotches.

Aunt Jean bent quickly to loosen the collar of the brown cape.

"Move back, everyone!" she ordered. "Let her get some air!"

"Must have been the strain of the journey," said Uncle Duncan. "The Atlantic is a pretty dangerous place these days. I'll call a doctor."

As he spoke, Lady Drume's eyelids fluttered. She slowly opened them and gazed up at the circle of faces above her.

"Goodness gracious! Dear, dear, dear!" she said uncertainly. "What happened?"

"You fainted, Lady Drume," answered Uncle Duncan. "Keep still," he added, as she began to struggle into a sitting position. "I am going to get a doctor."

"Nonsense!" Lady Drume said, "Never fainted before in my life! Just a touch of malaria, from the old days in India. Nothing to worry about! Help me up!"

She heaved herself to her feet, as they all hurried to help her. However, despite her brave words, Lady Drume looked shaken and uncertain. Uncle Duncan took charge.

"Whether it is malaria, or whether it is fatigue, you are not well enough to go on to Victoria today," he said. "We are going to take you home and have our doctor check you over!" He led Lady Drume gently but firmly to the car.

They soon left the city behind and headed west along the shore of a bay with mountains on the other side. Before long, the car climbed a long hill and turned into the driveway of a rambling house at the top. A large Airedale leaped at Sara's window excitedly, as the car pulled up at the front door.

"Don't be scared of Fearless!" called a tall boy of about thirteen who ran out to greet them. He was Sara's cousin, Jamie. Cousin Mary followed him.

Aunt Jean led Lady Drume straight up to bed, while the rest of them carried in the bags. Then Jamie grabbed Sara's arm.

"Come on!" he cried, "I've got a lot of stuff to show you. My snake and my Big Little Book collection. And the sailboat I'm building in the garage. And . . ."

Mary broke in, laughing. "Jamie, cut it out. The poor kid only just got here!"

"She wants to—don't you, Sara? After all that time in the train, I bet you want to break loose in a million directions, don't you?"

"Oh, yes," said Sara. "I do. Only . . . only I . . ."

"Jamie!" Aunt Jean came down the stairs. "Let Sara catch her breath, for heaven's sake! Go for a run with Fearless while I show Sara her room." Taking Sara by the hand, she led her to a little room on the third floor, at the top of the house.

"This is yours, my dear—I thought you'd like the breeze that comes in off the bay, and the view of Grouse Mountain on the other side. Now I think it would do you good to rest for a while. You look tired out. You've had quite a lot to get used to in a short space of time. So lie down for a bit and close your eyes. I'll come up for you later, honey."

Sara loved the room at once. And oh, how good it was to be alone again!

She went to the window. Leaning her aching head against the cool pane, she stared out at the humpbacked mountain across the bay. Grouse Mountain, Aunt Jean had called it. To Sara, it had a brooding look—somehow forbidding. The glare on the sparkling water below caused her to frown and blink, and she turned away and lay down on the bed, her head throbbing against the pillow. She was ill. And, kind as everyone was, she was lonely.

As Sara closed her eyes, she heard her aunt's voice in the hallway below.

"Duncan, there's no question that Lady Drume is really sick. She is going to have to stay with us for a while. She needs to be cared for."

"Dr. Archer will be able to tell us more when he gets . . ." Sara drifted off to sleep.

It was evening when she woke up. Aunt Jean was standing by her bed with a tray.

"Well," said Aunt Jean, shaking her head, "it looks to me as if I have two invalids to take care of!"

"Two?" asked Sara, feeling confused.

"Lady Drume has the measles, of all things! And, by the look of that rash on your face, I'd say you have, too. However did you two manage to catch the measles in the middle of the Atlantic?"

The measles! Sick though she was, Sara burst out laughing. Ernie and Maggie had got their revenge on Lady Drume!

Aunt Jean set out a light supper on her bedside table, while Sara told her about her two friends and how Lady Drume had had them taken off the Duke of Perth.

"I miss them a lot," she said. "They are the best friends I ever had. After Ann Palmerston, that is. We had such fun together. Supposing they get separated and sent to different homes!"

"I'll see if I can find out anything," promised Aunt Jean. "Perhaps we can get an address and you can write to them. But, for now, let's see if you can eat some of these scrambled eggs."

Sara tried to swallow some of the eggs, but her throat seemed to close against them. She lay down again. Below her, on the next floor, she could hear Lady Drume issuing orders and complaints in a steady flow.

Jamie stuck his head around the door and,

seeing that she was awake, came in. Fearless padded after him and, coming to the bedside, he laid his warm muzzle on the bed against her leg. If she had closed her eyes, she could have imagined it was Domino.

"Phew! What a dragon you've brought with you!" Jamie said. "She's got us all running in circles! How did you take it, all the way from England?" He grinned at her. "How're you feeling? Do you itch? I had measles a couple of years ago, and I felt rotten. Do you feel rotten?"

Sara nodded, then stopped nodding quickly. Even that motion seemed about to topple her head right off her shoulders.

Aunt Jean came in, carrying a bottle of medicine.

"Shoo, Jamie!" she ordered. "I want Sara to rest!"

"See you later," he whispered. "Come on, Fearless."

Sara felt happy inside. Jamie seemed to like her. She choked down the strong-tasting medicine and turned on her side to sleep. She slid down into velvet darkness, deep and close and warm. She lay curled at the bottom of a pit . . .

"Cut off the hair! We must all do our bit to

keep fit!" cried a voice. Lady Drume sat on the deck, a struggling Domino held fast in her lap. She was snipping away at his dense, shiny coat with a pair of garden shears. Fur cascaded like a fountain into a bucket at her feet. "Serves him right!" exclaimed Lady Drume. "That's what he gets for running around with alley cats!" Domino squirmed helplessly, his eyes piteous. Sara tried to spring forward to help him, but her legs would not move. As she watched, Lady Drume's face seemed to melt and run together and then reform. She was the mad Queen of Hearts. "Cut off her hair! Cut off her head! Cut off her hair! Cut off her head!" screeched the Queen of Hearts. Rising from her throne, she dropped Domino into the sea beside Ernie and Maggie, and advanced upon Sara.

"No!" screamed Sara. "Keep away from me!" She tried to cover her head with her arms and curled into a protective ball. "Don't cut my hair off! Don't! Don't!" She burst into tears, which became shrieks of terror, as the Queen of Hearts clutched her shoulder . . .

"Sara! Sara!" cried the Queen of Hearts. "Stop crying, child! I could hear you all the way down in my bedroom. Whatever is the matter?

162

Sara stared in horror at Lady Drume's face looming over her. "They're in the sea!" she sobbed. "They'll drown and I'll never see them again!"

"Ssh! There, Sara. It's all right, child! Oh, dear, dear, dear!" said Lady Drume and sat down heavily on the bed. "Goodness gracious! I had no idea!" She patted Sara's arm gently, until the wild fear eased out of Sara's thudding heart. "I should have thought you'd forgotten all about . . . what were their names?"

"Oh, Lady Drume," wept Sara. "I'll never forget Maggie and Ernie!"

Aunt Jean hurried into the room. "I knew I heard crying," she said, looking down at Sara. "Bad dream, honey? What a shame! Probably the medicine." She smoothed the covers and turned Sara's pillow to its cool side. "It'll soon be morning. Try to get back to sleep."

She turned to Lady Drume, her face serious. "You shouldn't be out of bed, Lady Drume. Measles are no laughing matter at our age. You could have fallen on the stairs. You should have called me!"

"No. I felt I had to come up myself, when I heard her weeping so," replied Lady Drume. "We've travelled a long way together, Sara and I."

EIGHTEEN
Homecoming

Three weeks passed slowly by in Sara's darkened bedroom. Each day, she asked, "Any letters for me?" But none came.

"Not yet, Sara," said Uncle Duncan. "Letters take a long time to get through these days."

Sara nodded, her lips set so that he would not see them tremble. He patted her hand where it gripped the bedclothes.

"I'm sure they've written, Sara," he said. "It's just that their letters have to be inspected by the censors and that takes time. And then, of course, military mail would take priority, if they're short of space." He hesitated. "There *is* the chance that their letters went down on their way over. There've been a lot more sinkings in the past couple of weeks. I hear they've stopped sending children across altogether, because the Atlantic's got so dangerous."

164

Sara turned her head away. She stared out at the evening sky, thinking of the news report she had heard that morning. She had been thinking about it all day.

"British Spitfire, Hurricane and Defiant fighters are engaging in constant aerial battle as German raiding activity near London increases. The third daylight attack on Dover occurred two days ago and, at last count, three hundred civilians have been killed. German dive-bombers have strafed several Kentish villages . . ."

She turned back to Uncle Duncan. "It's the not knowing that's the worst," she said.

"Well . . . no news is good news! That's the old saying, Sara!" said her uncle, gently.

Jamie came in. "You look better tonight," he said. "If you ask me, it's Mom who's going to end up in bed! She says Lady Drume is impossible. She won't do what the doctor tells her and she's grumpy all the time. I bet she thinks the measles is a German plot to keep her out of action!"

The next day, when Sara woke up, her head felt light and clear.

"Your rash is gone, Sara," said her aunt with satisfaction. "Lady Drume is better, too. She's planning to leave for her daughter's home tomorrow. I am going to let you both come downstairs to dinner tonight. We'll have a real Canadian meal to celebrate—salmon and corn on the cob and blueberry pie. And I've asked our neighbors, the Lloyds, to come with their children. We'll have a real party!"

"Can't I come down now?" Sara asked. "I've been up here so long and I haven't even seen the house or the garden or anything!"

"Just one more day, Sara. Rest quietly today to make sure."

Evening finally came. Sara was dressed and waiting when Mary put her head around the door at six o'clock.

"Ready?" she asked.

"Am I!"

"Okay. Let's go. Careful, now," cautioned Mary, holding onto her arm firmly. "You might be a bit wobbly after being in bed so long."

As they headed down the stairs, Fearless barked at the doorbell. "Let's hurry!" Sara said.

A boy's voice rose above the cheerful din.

"Coo-er! This is a bit of all right!"

"Shush! You didn't oughter say things like that!" a girl's voice interrupted.

Sara gasped. Letting go Mary's arm, she flew down the last flight of stairs. In a moment, she had flung her arms around Maggie's neck.

"I can't believe it!" she cried. "I can't believe my eyes! How did you get here?"

" 'Ere! Don't I get any attention?" complained Ernie.

Sara gave him a huge bearhug, to hide the tears in her eyes, and then whirled around to her aunt.

"How did you do it? How did you find them?"

"Oh . . . we did a bit of detective work. Didn't we, Lady Drume? And the Lloyds had room for them now their boys are in the Army. Now why don't you children amuse yourselves until dinner's ready?"

The three friends, with Jamie and Mary and Fearless as their guides, explored the house and the garden and the cliffwalk down to the beach. Then Sara took them up to the top of the house to see her room and to show them Grouse Mountain and the sailboats on the bay.

"We only just got 'ere today," said Ernie. "So we 'aven't seen anything yet."

"I haven't either—because of *your* measles!" Sara said, laughing. "But that doesn't matter. Because now we'll be able to see everything together."

"Mrs. Lloyd says we'll be at the same

school," Maggie said. "I'm so 'appy, Sara. And it's all thanks to Lady Drume, really."

"Lady Drume?"

"Well, according to what I 'eard, the people in charge at the center 'ad finally found a farm up north somewhere where we could both go. The farm workers 'ad left to join the Army and the farmer could use the extra 'ands. They reckoned that would be just the place for us. When your aunt got in touch with the children's center, they didn't want to change all their plans and send us to Vancouver instead. But old Lady D. got on the blower and give 'em what for—told 'em they'd better get us on a train to Vancouver or there'd be 'ell to pay! And 'ere we are! She don't take no for an answer!"

Sara spun about toward the door. "Wait here! I'll be back in a minute."

She found Lady Drume by the fireplace.

"Well, child. Do Ernie and Maggie like it here?"

"They love it, Lady Drume. We are all so happy. I don't think you could ever know how happy we are, but I wanted to tell you anyway."

Sara flung her arms around Lady Drume and hugged her hard. "Thank you. Thank you!"

She felt Lady Drume bend under her stiff corseting. Oh no! She's going to faint again! Sara thought wildly. But Lady Drume was bending to kiss the top of Sara's head.

"Well, well, Sara. That's all right, child," she said. "After all, I was the one who separated you. It seemed only right that I should be the one to bring you all together again. Only right!" She stroked Sara's hair, fine and glossy as a bird's wing.

Aunt Jean came in. "Dinner's ready," she said. "Where is everybody?"

"I'll get them," Sara said. She hugged Lady Drume once more and then ran upstairs to get the others.

Everything tasted wonderful. And after dinner the hours flew by, filled with talk and laughter and "remember when's". At last Mrs. Lloyd stood up to go.

"Come on, you two," she said to Maggie and Ernie. "You've had a big day."

"So have I," said Sara, her eyes shining.

After they had left, she looked for Lady Drume again. She found her standing by the window, looking across the bay.

"I . . . . I'll be leaving in the morning, Sara— probably before you get up. So I'll say good-bye now. And . . . and I hope you'll spare a thought for old Lady Drume every now and then . . ."

"Oh, Lady Drume, I'll never forget you! You're one of my best friends! I'll get up to say goodbye."

"Well, well, child," Lady Drume said gruffly. "Goodness me!" She cleared her throat. "I think I'd better pack my case," she said with her head turned away.

"I'll see you in the morning," Sara said.

She watched Lady Drume go up the stairs and then turned back to the window. The stars had come out above humpbacked Grouse Mountain. It loomed like black velvet against the sky. But it no longer looked forbidding.

Singing a little tune, she headed up the stairs toward her room.

"Why, Sara," said Aunt Jean behind her. "I do believe that's the first time in all these weeks I've heard you sing!"

Uncle Duncan put his arm around Sara's shoulders.

"Do you know what you remind me of, Sara?" he asked. "Something I haven't heard in a long time. You sound just like an English nightingale!"

EPILOGUE

Sara was thirteen before she saw England again.

She searched the crowd at the dock for the parents she remembered—her father tall above her in his Airforce blue—her mother soft-cheeked and bright-eyed. She had walked right past the thin graying couple at the barrier when the woman followed her and touched her arm.

"Sara?" her mother asked, uncertainly.